Praise for *A Wizard's Guide to Family Recovery*

"*A Wizard's Guide to Family Recovery* provides a novel and entertaining perspective on understanding and working through the extremely difficult, often gut-wrenching process of dealing with the addiction of a loved one. Lance Wilson utilizes historical and fictional characters in addressing the full spectrum of painful emotions that this real-life challenge brings up to create a solution-oriented path toward the goal of family recovery."

—**Dan Mager, MSW**
Author of *Roots and Wings: Mindful Parenting in Recovery* and *Some Assembly Required: A Balanced approach to Recovery from Addiction and Chronic Pain*

Hard truths are provided in an entertaining and lighthearted story covering the family dysfunction of addictive disorders and mental illness. Wilson delves into the codependent's dilemma of how much to do or not to do for their addicted loved ones and the need for self- focus rather than external focus. A well written journey through one of life's most significant challenges for many families.

—**George Kaiser M.D**
Fellow American Society of Addiction Medicine

A Wizard's Guide to Family Recovery is a book with words of wisdom for everyone – even those whose life has been untouched by addictions of any kind (if those people exist?). I especially like how Wilson wove the readings and writings of so many prominent authors and figures of history into a story whose characters spanned both great whimsy and pathos. Building humorous aspects into this often heartbreaking subject adds a valuable dimension as we need to find reasons to laugh regardless of what is happening around us. I highly encourage all looking for an insightful and fun read to pick up a copy of this book.

—**Ruth Huyler Glass**
Educator

"An absolutely brilliant approach to understanding the recovery process. This is the most unique approach I've seen in the many years I've been working with people in recovery. If you're considering entering recovery, this book will provide you with a solid path to start your journey on. A must read!"

—**Hugh Patterson**
Recovery and Chess Coach
Author of *Chess - Beginners & Intermediate; Openings, Strategies, & Endgames*

"As a judge who ran a drug court for several years, a premise of A Wizard's Guide to Family Recovery that families are impacted by a loved ones' addictions cannot be overstated. I have seen firsthand how addiction is a family disease. I appreciate how this book stresses the importance of family members addressing their trauma through their own recovery and the importance of group meetings in this process. As a chess player myself, I also agree that many lessons of this game can aid in growth and recovery, such as looking several moves ahead, patience, and learning to win and lose gracefully. I highly recommend a Wizard's Guide to Family Recovery to anyone impacted by addiction or other forms of mental illness, which is tragically far too many."

—**Judge Cedric A. Kerns, Retired**
Las Vegas Municipal Court

"This new book uses the game of chess to show the story of how a family is addressing mental health and addiction issues. The intersection is cleverly woven into the story and the dialogue. It is quietly effective in explaining tough issues. You needn't play chess or have a family to appreciate it. The dialogue is easy to follow and interestingly subtle."

—**Judge Nancy Allf, Retired**
Eighth Judicial District, Las Vegas, NV

"Merlin (Merlynn); Recovery; Chess. If this were an answer in Jeopardy's popular common bonds category, even the GOAT, Ken Jennings, would be stumped! Yet they work together in a unique way to guide the main character and the reader in learning techniques to cope with the challenges of codependency and to grow as a healthy person. Using quotes from chess grandmasters and addiction experts as well as reflections by a wise chess queen and her inquisitive pawn, we see a path to personal growth through group support, self-forgiveness and taking time to enjoy life. Wizard's Guide is an extensively researched and creative take on what could be a very dry subject. I learned a considerable amount and I enjoyed it!"

—**Sharon Dietz**
Lance Wilson's Junior High Chess Coach

Fun, informative, and clever. A perfect balance of prose and lessons in life. Wilson displays a masterful game using an invisible hand to control his characters and the meaning of their relationships as they move toward final resolution. Checkmate!

—**James W. McCormack**
Clerk of Court, Retired. United States District Court - Eastern District of Arkansas

"Lance's use of chess strategies as tools for recovery provides inspiration and reinforces a valuable life-changing lesson that chess is more than a game played on a board. It is a guide for making better choices and decisions in life. *A Wizard's Guide to Family Recovery* can help you find a way to use what you have to get what you want."

—**Chessman Eugene Brown**
Author of *From Pawns to Kings!*

Lance Wilson has taken an unconventional and, at times, lighthearted approach to deal with a serious issue that many of us have confronted: dealing with a family member's addiction or mental illness. Wilson's writing reveals the wisdom gained through his own experiences and shares lessons learned in a generous, insightful manner. Instead of sermonizing, the author engages the reader in a delightful and entertaining odyssey of discovery.

Mr. Wilson helps the reader comprehend that the solutions and answers we seek for loved one who are in pain are frequently elusive or unavailable. Yet we struggle and search! The real lesson of this book, perhaps, is that we should never give up and never abandon those we love, even when in their despair, they cannot reciprocate our caring or altruism. What we can really offer the victims of addiction or mental illness is our love and attention, letting them know they are never alone!

Lance Wilson has given us a gift for which we should be grateful.

—**Michael Eric Siegel, Ph.D**.
Adjunct professor of Government at Johns Hopkins University
and the author of *Lessons in Leadership from
the White House to Your House.*

A Wizard's Guide to Family Recovery

A Novel

Lance S. Wilson

Published by Starved Raccoon, LLC
Copyright © 2025 Lance S. Wilson

Copyright © 2025 Lance S. Wilson

All rights reserved. This book or any portion thereof may not be reproduced or used in any manner whatsoever without the express written permission of the publisher except for the use of brief quotations in a book review.

This book is a work of fiction. Names and characters are the product of the author's imagination and any resemblance to actual persons, living or dead, is entirely coincidental

ISBN – 9781734140323 (Paperback Edition)

ISBN – 9781734140330 (E-Book Edition)

Printed and Bound in the United States of America - First printing, 2025.

Cover Illustration by Brian Swanson - www.brianswansonstudio.com

Author photograph by Steve Patchin - www.patchinpictures.com

Published by – Starved Raccoon, LLC, Tucson, AZ

Preface

What

A Wizard's Guide to Family Recovery presents tools and strategies for those dealing with the emotional trauma caused by a loved one's addiction or other mental illness. Stated more boldly, if you choose to put some of these ideas to work for you, *A Wizard's Guide* promises turning uncertainty to acceptance, anger to equanimity, and hopelessness to hopefulness.

This may be a new genre of literature: fictionalized inspirational self-help, or FISH. To emphasize the importance of the first word, this *is* a work of fiction. And as fiction, nothing in *A Wizard's Guide* should be taken as medical advice or professional counseling. If you are struggling with any of the issues identified herein, please seek professional help from a certified medical professional or counselor.

Most of the stories in this book are based on both my experiences and lessons I learned from others. Historical fiction may apply here as well: some of my depictions of real people are largely based on actual events. I've taken artistic license with settings and situations, but, for the most part, quotations are accurate to the best of my understanding.

Shifting to the inspirational self-help side of this genre mash-up, as the characters of *A Wizard's Guide* share stories and work on their own growth, they explore topics including codependency, the symptoms of addiction, *both/and* thinking, family structures, embracing uncertainty and forgiveness, and the value of support groups.

This book takes an admittedly unconventional and sometimes lighthearted—even irreverent—approach to its heartbreaking subject matter. It does so because through hard work, therapy, peer support, and internal examination, people can find reasons for hope, reasons to laugh, and reasons to celebrate life as they work through challenging times.

Who

What are my qualifications to write *A Wizard's Guide to Family Recovery*? First, to show I still need to work on my own codependency, I will begin with what I am not. I am not a psychologist, a chess grandmaster, a well-known author, or, unfortunately, a wizard.

To quell those disclaimers: I bring unique and relevant experience to this topic and an unbridled passion for helping others. To start, I am an adult child of an alcoholic. My father committed suicide when I was twelve years old. The disease of alcoholism had defeated him. It accomplished its primary mission of killing the person with the disease, while devastating those impacted by its evil, long-reaching tentacles.

In the following weeks, months, and years, I did as many children unfortunately do in situations like this: I took on responsibility for something I had no right or rational reason to claim as my own. I connected dots I never should have connected. I assumed my father's suicide was somehow my fault. Through many years of therapy and group sessions, I now know my crappy grades in eighth grade did nothing to worsen his illness. More likely, his illness and death that year had something to do with my worsening grades.

I also bring to this book the experience of having a loved one who suffers from a schizoaffective disorder. Though upsetting, this experience gave me a deeper understanding of mental illnesses and the grief of ambiguous loss. To be clear, growing up in a home with an alcoholic parent and having a loved one with mental illness has not defined who I am. I refuse to be a victim of past circumstances. My life has been full of many wonderful blessings. I am thankful for the numerous, varied chapters of my years on this planet, and, yes, even the darker and more challenging ones, as they have resulted in much learning and personal growth.

Why

Hopefully, the *Who* section above provides reasons behind my inspiration to write about family recovery. While my and your experiences with mental illnesses are unique, such experiences are also sadly far too common for far too many people. I encourage others to share their stories as well.

The novel approach of making Merlynn the Wizard a main character of this book and incorporating a chess theme requires further explanation. It felt natural that Merlynn serve as a main character, as I've been fascinated by the wizard's magical powers since I first saw the movie *Camelot* in eighth grade. I fell more deeply in love with these tales after reading T. H. White's *The Once and Future King* in high school. The noble goal of King Arthur's Round Table—that of championing right over might—resonated with me and still does. Building Merlynn into the narrative of *A Wizard's Guide* also permitted a fantasy element I found entertaining.

As for chess, the game was a lifeline for me during high school and college when I still thought I was responsible for my alcoholic father's suicide. It was the one thing I was good at. Chess gave me a sense of identity that otherwise would have been lost in the shadows of codependency. Through chess, I learned patience, critical thinking, planning, humility, and other important life skills. Throughout *A Wizard's Guide*, I use chess principles as examples of ways to build recovery skills in the hope it will encourage you to take up this daunting and rewarding game—or, if you already play, to revisit its principles as an entry point to recovery.

By sharing my life experiences and channeling what I have learned from many wonderful people through my own recovery, I hope that *A Wizard's Guide To Family Recovery* may be of service to those in need. I have no idea how many moves I have left on the amazing chess board of life as I approach my own endgame. If this book helps a few others navigate their own games and move their pieces with grace and dignity, it will have been well worth the time and energy to write.

—Lance S. Wilson

Prologue
by Merlynn

My name is Merlynn. You likely have seen my name spelled *Merlin* or possibly *Merlyn*, the British version. I am fine with any spelling of my name as long as I am represented properly as the wise necromancer I am. I use the version with two *n*'s at the end when I take the form of a female, which I do here. In this story, I am an ancient, beautifully hand-carved emerald-green queen in a chess set. I am also the same wizard you likely first heard of through the King Arthur tales.

Many have questioned whether there is historical documentation for the King Arthur tales—for Camelot, Guinevere, Lancelot, the Round Table, and the various quests of the colorful characters portrayed therein. The short answer to this question is no: there is no historical evidence any of those characters ever existed. That said, there can be no doubt that *I* exist, as I am writing this prologue.

To quote someone else for whom there is questionable historical evidence, father of Taoism Lao Tzu: "When the student is ready, the teacher appears." I operate mostly on that principle. If someone is ready for what I have to offer them, I will appear. I may even have been with you in the past, as I often opt not to make my presence known.

If you are having a hard time accepting the above, I ask that you look through the eyes of a young child. Children have marvelous senses of wonder and imagination—which, sadly, usually disappear as they grow up. I find this to be tragic. Ask yourself: When did you stop skipping? When do children stop skipping? Perhaps we stop skipping when the magic of mystery leaves us. If that is the case for you, I hope *A Wizard's Guide* brings the skip back into your step and reignites your inner child.

Please permit me to introduce the other three main characters who share the stage with me in this story. The first is someone I've grown to be extremely fond of. Her name is Queen's Pawn or simply QP. She is the pawn who sits in front of me on the board at the beginning of a game. QP has been with me in this chess set for several centuries, but it is only at the beginning of this story that QP becomes aware. *Becoming aware* is a term I use whenever I bring something else to life.

The other two main characters are humans: Arnie and Michael. I have known Arnie for approximately ten years, as that is how long he has been in possession of the chess set in which QP and I reside. I will meet Michael for the first time soon. I know this because I am aging backward and have already lived through the future. And, yes, this confuses even me.

I must end this prologue, as the story is about to begin. QP and I are in the chess set on the back seat of Arnie's car, and he will soon take us inside the Becoming Aware Recovery Center (BARC). I will close by emphasizing the need for all of us to stay life-long learners. To stay curious. To stay fully engaged in life. And, to have fun on the journey. I hope you learn something as you embark on this quest with me—a learning quest in which the quarry is equanimity, and once it is found, one can never dream of regretting.

Chapter 1

As Michael Weed drove his pickup truck through town toward the Becoming Aware Recovery Center (BARC), he had no idea he would soon come into the presence of an actual wizard.

Though unaware of this new, mysterious force he'd soon encounter, Michael did know Goofus all too well. As Michael turned into the recovery center's parking lot, Goofus jumped up and down on his left shoulder and screamed, "Turn around! There's nothing wrong with you! Go home! You don't need this kind of meeting!"

Goofus stopped his jumping and tried pleading. "Drive right by this place. Don't stop. This isn't for you. You don't have to be here. Come on, Michael, you don't use alcohol ... or any drugs, for that matter. This place is for low-life losers, hookers, ex-cons. We don't belong here. It's a waste of time."

Goofus didn't know the old red-brick building was a place of respite for people in need of support and guidance for a variety of emotional and mental challenges, not just those suffering from addiction.

The troublemaker slumped inside his typical slob attire and ceased his constant blabbering long enough for his arch nemesis, Gallant, to weigh in.

Gallant, Michael's gentle and thoughtful angel, neatly dressed and perched on his right shoulder, weighed in, "Michael, when has listening to Goofus ever been good for you? Remember when he told you to get in your dad's truck at the top of the steep driveway, put it in neutral, and release the emergency brake? At least you weren't hurt. Only Goofus thought it was funny. Your father certainly didn't laugh. How much did that tow truck cost, anyway?"

Michael agreed that had been a dumb thing to do, even if he'd been only six years old at the time. Dad hadn't been drinking too much that day, fortunately, so his punishment wasn't as severe as it could have been. He also had to agree with Gallant that listening to Goofus seldom ended well. Goofus' impulses often felt more fun in the short term but were hardly beneficial in the long run.

Gallant persisted. "Are you sleeping well, Michael? Are you content with your current situation? Is it working for you? Are you at peace? I think if you're honest with yourself, you have to say no. So what do you have to lose? Park the truck and take a chance on this place!"

***

Michael somewhat reluctantly agreed with the wiser Gallant, parked his truck, and contemplated entering the recovery center. He chuckled to himself. At forty-five, he was the hardworking entrepreneur and owner of Weed No More lawn service. He often got calls at work from parents looking for some magic formula to stop their kids from smoking marijuana. Had the name of his company been a good idea? After all, Goofus had suggested it.

Michael was busy during the summer months, with four crews working from dawn to dusk to keep neighborhood lawns looking great. He had scant lawn business during the cold, shorter winter days in Marietown, Pennsylvania, so he stayed busy as a handyman for his many clients.

He'd had a difficult childhood. His dad's drinking often disrupted family plans. His birthday parties typically became disasters, Dad falling down drunk or doing something else to end the party early. After Michael's thirteenth birthday party, these disasters stopped. They were replaced by the disaster of Dad putting a gun to his head and pulling the trigger a few days after Christmas.

Michael's mother had done her best to offset the devastating effects caused by this type of childhood trauma. She'd bucked the unfortunate trend of the time: keeping secrets and not openly discussing the illness of addiction. Instead, she had shared honestly with Michael about his father's illness and tried her best to raise a healthy, confident son. Despite her efforts, Michael still suffered many of the damaging traits of being an adult child of an alcoholic.

As he sat in his truck in BARC's ice-covered parking lot, he still had no idea what to expect. The flyer he'd seen at the grocery store said this place offered services for family members of addicts and those in turmoil over any loved one with a similar mental illness. Clearly that fit his past and current experiences, but he still hesitated. He'd never been to such a place and couldn't fathom sharing ugly family secrets with a bunch of strangers. One thing Michael did know for sure: he needed a good night's sleep, something that had eluded him for many, many months. He was so very tired.

Michael wiped his tired eyes and told the still-sniveling Goofus to shut up.

***

What the hell I am doing? Michael thought as he walked through the darkness toward the building. Studying the door and deep in thought, he didn't see the patch of ice beneath him and suddenly found himself flat on his back. Fortunately, his ego was the only thing bruised—though the bruise on his ego got a bit larger as he heard a low chuckle from the shadow-cloaked figure getting out of a car in the handicapped spot next to the front entrance.

"Hey, you okay?" asked Arnold Zugzwang, better known to his friends as Arnie, as he tried to suppress his laughter.

"Yep, just a bit rattled." Michael got up, brushed himself off, and tiptoed slowly over the ice toward the stranger's voice.

"Well, if we weren't a little rattled, we wouldn't need to be here, would we?" Arnie said.

Now a few feet from the stranger, Michael noticed the man reaching for something through the open back door of his old wood-paneled station wagon, the other hand on his cane.

"Do you need some help there?" Michael asked.

"Yes, please. Could you reach in and get this dang thing for me? I think my arms are shrinking along with my height."

Michael was glad to be of assistance to this gentleman, who he'd soon learn was eighty years old. He reached into Arnie's back seat and grabbed a worn, coffee-stained, green-zippered cloth case. As he grabbed the case, he felt a strange sensation, like a tingling in his arm. He wrote this off to having just fallen. Nerve pain, maybe.

"Is there a pool cue in here? I may come in after all. I love to shoot pool!"

"No, it's a chess set," Arnie said. "Unfortunately, BARC doesn't have a pool table, though I wish they did. But hey, what's this about not coming in?" With that, he extended his free hand and said, "Arnold Zugzwang, but my friends call me Arnie. And now you are one of my friends, so please call me that."

"Great to meet you, Arnie." As they exchanged a firm handshake, Michael wondered how to respond to Arnie's question about his hesitation to come inside. "This is my first time here," he said. "I don't see how I would fit in. I'm just not sure I need a place like this."

Having been around the center more years than he cared to recall, Arnie had heard many newcomers share similar reservations.

"Well, if you leave now, that swan dive you not so elegantly performed a minute ago would be for nothing, right?" he said with his usual lightheartedness, the sparkle in his eyes now evident to Michael. "We have strong, tasty hot coffee and this is also our holiday celebration, so there'll be plenty of snacks. Besides, I need help with the door, so you're sort of stuck now, aren't you?"

"You got me there."

As he held the door open for Arnie, Michael was still fighting the urge to go back to his truck. Despite that urge, he entered BARC—and so began a new adventure, one that would be heart-wrenching, scary, hopeful, and rewarding, but never boring.

Chapter 2

As Michael entered BARC, he heard a voice call out from behind the reception desk.

"Arnie, you old dog! Long time since last month. Who's this with you?"

As Michael would soon find out, the voice belonged to Brandon Artlove, the recovery center's director of programs. Brandon had flowing hair well below his shoulders, a solid chin one would expect on a movie star, and gentle eyes.

He turned toward Michael. "I trust you're here for the family support meeting, since that's all we've got going on tonight. Have you been here before?"

"Nope, this is my first time." Every muscle in Michael's body still readied to turn and flee despite the warm greeting.

He stood, arms folded, eyes darting around the room. On the wall to his left he saw a beautiful painting with vivid colors and bold strokes. A painting of one of his favorite jam bands, Goose, one of many jam bands Michael listened to but had never seen live.

Brandon noticed Michael's diverted attention. "I see you staring at that painting. Do you like it?"

"Yeah, I love it. They're one of my favorite bands."

"Mine too, which is why I took a shot at painting them," said Brandon, somewhat sheepishly.

Michael unfolded his arms and smiled. He felt an instant connection to this guy who seemed perfectly at ease letting his freak flag fly.

"Welcome. I'm Brandon, Brandon Artlove. I hang out here a lot. Let me show you around, as I know this guy"—he glanced at Arnie—"needs to get to the coffee pot before we start the meeting so he can stay awake at his advanced age."

"Bug off, you long-haired freak," Arnie huffed as he headed into the break room, where Michael glimpsed a few aging vending machines, four Formica-covered metal tables, several chairs with pieces of cardboard tucked under certain legs for balance, and the all-important coffee station.

"Artlove, and you paint," Michael said as he extended his hand toward Brandon. "Michael Weed."

Brandon laughed. "Wow, Weed. And you think my last name is funny. Are you sure you're here for the right meeting?" They both chuckled, and Michael started to feel more at home. Maybe this wasn't such a bad idea. He was glad he'd ignored Goofus.

Except Goofus was right about one thing: Michael *had* never had a problem with alcohol or other drugs. He didn't suffer from addiction or the mental health challenges other people faced.

Though Michael didn't know it yet, it was far from the truth to say he had nothing to recover from. As a matter of fact, he did have a brain disease: codependency, an illness that could be just as deadly as any other if left untreated.

Brandon walked Michael around narrow, scuffed, paint-chipped passages that had seen better days. He explained the various programs BARC offered there while Michael struggled to stay focused.

"We are fortunate to have five meeting rooms so we can have numerous sessions going on at the same time," Brandon said. "And, trust me, while I think most in this community could benefit from so many meetings, we usually only have one or two meetings every evening and a few more on Saturdays when people are off work."

I don't even want to be here on a Wednesday night, Michael couldn't help thinking. *Why the heck would someone come here on their day off?*

He could feel the walls start to close in on him. His breathing became jagged; the saliva in his mouth dried up. He wanted to turn around and run as fast as he could to the exit.

Instead, he asked, "Sorry if this sounds stupid, but ... I've heard of meetings for alcoholics and addicts, but why would you need *five* meeting rooms?"

"Good question," Brandon said. "While those are, unfortunately, very common problems many of our clients—no, let's call them friends—struggle with, that's only the tip of the iceberg. People face many different traumas. Meeting with other like-minded people in the community often helps them find the support they so desperately need. Many members find strength in numbers and comfort, knowing they're not alone.

"See, this room is where people with eating disorders meet on Friday nights. Oh, and right across the hall we often have meetings for those with obsessive-compulsive disorders. And this sign here is left over from last night, when we needed to let people know we moved the sex addiction meeting to room C because we had a leak in our old roof again."

Upon hearing the word *sex*, Goofus prepared to launch into one of his highly inappropriate and immature comments. Thankfully, before he could utter some crude nonsense, Gallant, knowing Goofus all too well, crawled over Michael's neck and planted a foot cleanly and firmly on Goofus'privates. "Don't even think about it," whispered Gallant. "Sex addiction is a manifestation of the disease of addiction, so be quiet. It can destroy lives the same way as addictions to alcohol or other drugs."

Brandon continued, unaware of the well-deserved assault that had just taken place on this newcomer's shoulder. "These two rooms are occupied by NAMI."

"What's that?"

"NAMI stands for the National Alliance on Mental Illness. They hold many different meetings, some here and some over Zoom. And they have a part-time staff person and volunteers who often use these rooms as well."

"I had no idea all of this even existed!" Michael said.

"Here's the meeting you're going to tonight, the once-a-month family support meeting," Brandon said. "I sure wish we had enough interest to hold this one every week, if not every night. It's hard to guess how many people could benefit from being here for this meeting, but I know the need out there is huge. These meetings could give a lot of hope to anyone who has a loved one with addiction issues or other mental health problems, or anyone who grew up in a dysfunctional family. And, sadly, I think that applies to most of us if we're truly honest with ourselves."

"I get the other meetings," Michael said. "But if family members don't suffer with addiction or the other stuff you just said, I guess I just don't understand how this meeting can help."

Brandon placed his hand on Michael's shoulder, unaware he was squishing Goofus, who was still curled up in a ball withering in pain. "You'll have a better understanding soon. And as you'll hear at the end, keep coming back."

***

The ninety-minute meeting passed more quickly than Michael expected. Unlike many of BARC's other free support group meetings run by volunteers, this one was led by a licensed counselor, Megan.

After welcoming all, Megan began by reviewing ground rules for the evening like those followed by most circles of trust: keeping everything said in the room confidential, refraining from trying to fix other people, always being respectful, and sharing honestly if moved to do so.

As Michael would come to learn, the meeting usually followed the same format. It started with a general discussion, led by Megan, about a topic related to family recovery or mental illness. The second half of the meeting was an opportunity for attendees to share whatever was going on with them at the moment and to gain insights from other attendees.

The topic for the educational component of tonight's meeting was codependency. Michael didn't think he'd ever heard the word before Megan explained it.

"Let's start by taking a look at a definition of *codependency*," she said. "I say *a* definition, as there are many different interpretations of this term."

She took a book from her briefcase. "I like this definition by Melody Beattie in her book *Codependent No More*: 'A codependent person is one who has let another person's behavior affect him or her, and who is obsessed with controlling that person's behavior.'[1] If you want to learn more about this topic, I highly recommend Ms. Beattie's book. She is one of the early pioneers to write about codependency, and this book contains a wealth of information."

With this, a woman a few seats away from Michael said, "If anyone wants a copy of *Codependent No More*, I have six with me tonight. I provide them for free as a way of saying thanks to everyone here at BARC. Please come see me after the meeting if you would like one."

"Thank you, Mary," Megan said. "It's so kind of you to offer those. I'm also handing around a list of some codependency traits that we'll use as a guide for our discussion tonight."

Megan reviewed the items on this handout: a tendency to do more than one's share, fear of abandonment and rejection, problems making decisions, poor communication in relationships, and others. After she concluded the educational portion of the meeting, some of the twenty or so people seated around the circle shared a little about why they were there, current challenges they were facing, and their progress in their own recovery.

The beads of sweat on Michael's head evaporated when he heard sharing was optional. He didn't want to speak in front of so many strangers. Megan explained that unlike in many group meetings, she would not go around the room asking people if they wanted to speak. Rather, they would start by sitting quietly until someone was moved to speak.

As Michael's first-ever support group meeting concluded, he heard a familiar voice over his shoulder. "Hey, Mr. Parking Lot Swan Dive, I have no one to help me put this chess set to use tonight. I sure hope you have time for a game?"

"I am pretty jacked up with sugar from all the holiday treats I just stuffed in my gut, so I'm not tired," Michael said. "A bit confused about what I just heard, but not tired. I hardly know how to play chess, though."

"Even better. Let's play for money, then," Arnie said.

Brandon, who was right behind them putting chairs back in order, gently smacked Arnie on the back of his shoulder. "Hey, you old codger, do you need to come back tomorrow for our Gamblers Anonymous meeting? No betting in this house, pal." He turned to Michael. "Don't let this old guy sucker you into playing for money. He's pretty good at chess and an even better teacher. Very patient. I mean, he taught me to play, so he can teach anyone. And he has much wisdom to share, so please stay if you have time. In a weaker moment, I gave Arnie a key, so he can lock up after he takes you to the cleaners—which shouldn't take long."

"Sure, I will stay for a bit." Michael said, smiling at Arnie and Brandon's playful relationship. "I have no reason to go home. I don't even like being there. Plus, I hardly sleep anyway, so why not?"

Arnie, with his keen insight, tucked away Michael's comment about not wanting to be home. He'd address that at a later time.

The two men moved down the hall to BARC's break room, where Arnie unpacked his chess set.

Chapter 3

The sound of Arnie unzipping his chess carrying case awoke the beautifully hand-carved emerald-green queen from her nap. Merlynn welcomed the breath of fresh air that entered The Cocoon as the light hit her. She had named this plush black velvet bag "The Cocoon" several centuries earlier.

It was here, in this chess bag, that Merlynn often reflected upon what she'd heard while she'd been in play. At other times, she rested. These tranquil times in The Cocoon helped her rejuvenate and blossom, become something richer and more beautiful: like a caterpillar morphing into a pupa, then emerging and soaring as a beautiful butterfly.

But this time, as all thirty-two pieces were brought out from the bag, it happened: the thing Merlynn had hoped for some time now. Arnie grabbed her and a pawn at the exact same time. In the seconds that Merlynn and this pawn—named QP, short for Queen's Pawn—were together in Arnie's hand, Merlynn took advantage of the wonderful coincidence and anointed the little pawn "aware."

Merlynn had significant powers, but with limitations. For instance, she could only bring another chess piece into awareness—or "to life"—when she and that piece were touched by a human at the same time. Now, the opportunity was here, and Merlynn jumped at it like a knight's surprise attack over another unsuspecting piece.

Meanwhile, QP felt a bolt shoot though her smoothly carved body and a rush of knowledge.

Merlynn knew she had but a year or so left until she'd no longer be able to communicate with anyone—aging backward as she was—and she wanted someone to carry on her teaching when she could no longer do so. So in this fleeting moment, she transferred many skills to the now blossoming QP. They

11

were skills—language, curiosity, reason, and critical thinking, to name a few—that would take years to develop, normally, but now time was of the essence. That's how, in a mere few seconds, QP leaped further ahead in knowledge than many humans who'd believed themselves "aware" for years.

Had Merlynn not felt this time crunch, she would have left QP to develop these abilities over time. She'd come to regard trial and error as a superior approach to learning than the one she now took. She knew the easy way out often led back in, yet today she took shortcuts.

In fact, in her haste—and likely because she was a bit befuddled—Merlynn had made a major mistake. When she attempted to imbue the little pawn with a sense of independence, she messed up the first two letters in the word. Rather than starting *independence* with the letters *in-*, Merlynn mistakenly started the word with *co-*. What a difference two letters can make!

Thus, our newly hatched little pawn started her journey with codependency firmly embedded in her blossoming brain, instead of the confidence of independence Merlynn had intended. No sooner was she aware than QP was instilled with damaging traits of codependency that would normally take years to develop—and only with enough negative influence from others.

***

QP looked around, observing everything for the first time and trying to make sense of the gift of knowledge Merlynn had just given her. To each side she noted objects shaped exactly like her, all lined up in a row, three to her right and four to her left. Across from her, another perfect line of identically shaped figures—except these were a little different, as they were a lighter color. Behind these stood eight other figures in varied sizes and shapes—but all taller than her.

As QP sized up the other figures, someone spoke. "The white pieces always move first, so go ahead, Michael," came the voice from above.

Another voice—QP assumed this one must be Michael's—responded, "Okay. I know how the pieces move but not much more, so please go easy on me, Arnie."

Curiously, QP heard what the humans were saying despite having no visible ears on her vacant bulb of a face. She didn't know yet she could not communicate with humans in any way. (Merlynn, on the other hand, as a queen, had a finely carved face with small ears. She also heard what humans said, but, unlike QP, the wizard queen could transmit thoughts to humans. She used this power very sparingly, however. It was important, she thought, to let people sort out their own issues and learn through their own experiences and mistakes.)

"No worries," Arnie said. "This is just a friendly game, and, more importantly, a time to chat. You'll figure out soon I love to talk. I hope you don't get sick of it, but I often share things I've read or learned about chess and how they helped me get through tough times. Is it okay if I share one of these thoughts before we get started?"

"Of course," Michael said. "I have a lot to learn, both about this game and what's going on at this place."

"Great. And please, if I ever get too long-winded, tell me. One thing to keep in mind when playing chess is never to play a move without a reason. This idea may help each time you consider what move to make. Actually, remembering this tip helps me to pause and think about my next move before jumping in, both in the game of chess and outside these walls. I always try to stop and look around and consider the likely outcome of what I do."

Arnie paused, then spoke again. "Chess has been used as a recovery tool for addicts in many settings. I've heard of places with cognitive training programs that use chess to help those in recovery regain attention span and memory functions that were damaged due to drug use. The game is also a great teacher of patience and graceful acceptance of loss."

With that, QP looked up and saw Michael's hand lift a figure just like her (but creamy white) and set it down, almost right across from her but off to the side a step. As she shook off the cobwebs of centuries of unconsciousness, her surroundings became clear to her. Yes, the very basics of chess were among the information Merlynn had time to teach her a few moments earlier when she became aware.

She was a pawn.

All of a sudden, a hand much more wrinkled than Michael's grabbed another green pawn right next to her and moved it up to face the lighter-colored pawn. "This is a very common opening, Michael," she heard. "One in which both players move their king pawns up two spaces. This helps free up other pieces and builds the ability to control the center of the board. Yes, a common chess opening indeed."

"What do you mean by 'opening'?" Michael asked. "And saying this one's very common? Are there a bunch of different ways to start a chess game?"

"Yes," Arnie said. "An infinite number of ways, likely. As for the term 'opening,' chess is often described in three phases: an opening, a middle game, and an ending. There is no firm definition of when one phase ends and the other begins. That often depends on the positions of pieces and the number of pieces left on the board."

"Wow," Michael said. "I never thought about that. I'd better just resign now. I hope my questions don't seem too dumb?"

"No worries," Arnie said. "I love explaining this game. About the openings ... I have no idea how many there are. As a much younger man, I often studied a book on *just* openings. *Chess Openings: Theory and Practice.* At least 750 pages. I still have it on a shelf at home. I can lend it to you if you like."

"Let's get through this game first."

"Got ya," Arnie said. "Okay, sorry, here I go again getting sidetracked with other thoughts as we start to play. I mentioned opening up the center of the board, the way we did when we played these two pawns. Staying centered is a theme you'll likely hear in meetings here at BARC. I try to keep that in mind—staying centered—when I'm playing this game and in my interactions in life. Or, to put it another way, I try to avoid the edges of the board where my moves may be more limited, just as I try to avoid limiting my options in life."

"Arnie the philosopher. Cool," Michael chimed in. "As I said, I know how the pieces move. And I know it's important to protect your king from being checkmated. Other than that, are some pieces considered worth more than others?"

Oh crap, here we go, Merlynn thought. *Don't you dare bring up piece rankings.* She knew doing so would only damage QP's young and impressionable psyche.

"Well, yes, sort of," Arnie said. "Technically, there aren't points assigned to each piece, but many chess players think of it this way: a king is priceless, a queen is worth nine points, a rook five points, bishops and knights about three points each—with a bishop being just a bit more valuable than a knight—and a pawn is worth one point."

One point? One lousy freaking point!? With that seemingly harmless passing comment, QP's codependency took a firmer hold on her. It was the first negative message to permeate her thought process. It went something like this: *I am not worth as much as others. I am disposable. I am not as important as the other pieces.*

***

Merlynn knew she had much work ahead of her to get these messages out of little QP's still young mind. As the game went on, she used the time to think about the best way to talk to QP about the feelings she was positive the newly aware little pawn would voice once they were returned to The Cocoon.

Merlynn hated this stupid way so many humans ranked the values of chess pieces. In her not-so-humble opinion, they were missing the most important aspect of the game of chess: the synergy and relationships among pieces depending on their positions on the board.

While Merlynn pondered how to address all this with QP, she was easily distracted. She soon started daydreaming about some of her ancient memories: some she'd had as a chess queen and some she'd had when she lived in other forms. She thought back on her most well-documented honor: she'd been a mentor to King Arthur, even before the king's royal heritage was known to anyone other than herself.

As part of young Arthur's education, Merlynn had turned him into several different animals. As she reflected on the time she turned Arthur into a fish, she recalled a discussion she felt might help when she talked with QP back in The Cocoon.

Upon becoming a fish, Arthur had begged Merlynn to accompany him. She'd said to him: "For this once, I will come. But in the future, you will have to go by yourself. Education is experience, and the essence of experience is self-reliance."[1] She was thankful she'd recalled this lesson. QP would have to learn self-reliance just as Arthur had.

Merlynn snapped back to the present as Arnie's hand grabbed her crown to move her to a better position on the board. She hoped she would remember this speech she'd given the young Arthur when it came time to talk to QP about the young pawn's insecurities.

15

Chapter 4

As Arnie moved his queen, he queried his new friend on his thoughts now that he'd attended his first family support meeting.

"Well, Michael, I enjoyed that meeting, and I hope you did, too. I think it was good for your first meeting that we started by reviewing this handout about codependency before we moved into time for individual sharing. What do you think?"

"My head is sort of spinning with too much new info. I liked the people around the circle. They all seemed nice. But, man, that one guy who said he was sort of glad he had an addict in his life because he'd grown so much in the past year? I couldn't help thinking that dude must be nuts."

"Fair, but he's far from crazy," Arnie said. "I get what he meant. I've said similar things myself in the past. Of course no one would actually wish for addicts or people with other mental illnesses in their lives. But stuff like this can lead to great growth, especially if we surround ourselves with others who have been through similar experiences and are willing to look at life as a learning opportunity." He paused. "Can I tell you a bit about why I'm here?"

"Hell no!" screamed the disheveled little Goofus into Michael's ear. "I've had enough of this place already. I'm sick of all this *blah, blah, blah*. Let's get out of here!"

Fortunately, Gallant's contrary message, "Ignore that mean little jerk wad," carried the day.

"Sure, I'd like to know why you're here, seeing as I still have no idea why I am. Other than meeting you, I mean. That's been fun."

"Thank you. The feeling is mutual. And give it time. You're not alone in your feelings as you start this new journey. I started coming here because my

17

wife of thirty-two years was an alcoholic. I stayed with her, but it was really hard. I lost her to liver failure a while back."

"Oh man, so sorry. That must have been really hard."

"For sure—and even harder before I found this place. While I wish things had been different, of course, I have no regrets. Well, some. But regrets are sort of a waste of time anyway, like the 'shoulda, woulda, coulda' mind trap we can easily get stuck in."

They'd been making chess moves during this discussion, and Michael now surprised Arnie by jumping his knight over another piece and capturing his opponent's queen's pawn. As he did so, he moved QP off to the side of the board close to the edge of the table.

Without warning, QP had become a mere observer for the rest of the game. Having just been made aware and still very young and vulnerable, she now felt more acutely her earlier feeling that, as a pawn, she was dispensable. Merlynn sensed this and knew it would only make her task to help QP overcome her insecurities even more daunting.

"Did this stuff—these meetings and being around others, I mean—did it help your wife get better?" Michael said. "That's why I'm here. I really need to learn how to fix my kids. One is an addict and the other has something going on in his head that I don't understand. He hears voices and just makes no sense at all. I haven't even seen him for over a year. I'm not even sure where he is or whether he's alive or dead. I need to know what I can do to change them. Is there a special meeting for that?"

Arnie had heard similar questions from others as they first entered BARC's doors. Newcomers often arrived looking for answers to whatever traumas they faced. While the circumstances varied from person to person, coming here with the goal of fixing loved ones was a common and understandable desire. While he'd addressed this wish several times, he knew the importance of his response and took time to focus on his next move on the board as he also thought about what to say.

"First, I'm so sorry you're having these issues with your kids," he said. "I hear you, and I know how hard that must be. You've hit on something very important in your question. It's a question I hear from most people when they first arrive here. And one I truly understand. Sadly, it doesn't have an easy answer. So please bear with me.

"No, there's no meeting here that can help you fix your children. Actually, there's no meeting here—or anywhere I know of—that can help you fix anyone else. I wish there were, because I'd write a book about it, get rich, and get rid of that old jalopy of mine you helped me grab this old chess set from earlier tonight. You may not want to hear this, but this whole place is about fixing you, not anyone else."

Michael heard this but hardly, as Goofus jumped up and down with glee and screamed in his ear. "Blah, blah, blah! Here we go with the psychobabble gobbledygook. I told you not to pull in here!" He laughed and blew Gallant a raspberry.

Gallant spoke up. "Michael, listen to this Arnie guy. You like him, right? Again, what do you have to lose? Give this a chance. Keep asking questions. Don't give up now!"

"Sorry, but I don't get it," Michael said. "I don't use drugs, and I'm not homeless on the street like my son because he won't get help. I just want them to get better. That's why I'm here! I love both my kids ..." Tears welled up in his eyes, he felt so helpless and exhausted.

Arnie reached across the table and placed his hand gently on Michael's sleeve to comfort him. As he did so, he accidently knocked QP off the edge of the table. QP bounced four or five times on the hard linoleum floor before hitting the wall and landing in a cold pool of coffee someone had spilled earlier. Merlynn winced.

What the fuck, thought QP. *Here I am, already set aside, useless, and I get knocked down and wind up here!* (Sorry about the language. It seems that when Merlynn brought QP into awareness, she failed to teach her about not swearing. Of course, Goofus was ecstatic at these recent developments and let his own string of profanities fly.)

"Michael, I know this is very hard, and I just threw a lot at you," Arnie said. "The tough truth is there are no easy fixes for what you're going through. All I ask for now is that you go easy on yourself and give this place a chance.

"While I don't claim to know much, one thing I have seen over the years is that those who keep coming back here tend to find this place helpful. The situations with their loved ones, whatever it is, may not change, but they have changed for the better."

"How could I change if my kids don't get better?" Michael asked.

"Well," Arnie said, "I've seen people who keep coming back start to smile again, laugh again, do fun things for themselves, and start to sleep better."

Michael wiped the tears from his eyes and found himself with no words. This was all too much for one night. He felt deflated. He just wanted to get up and leave. Arnie had sensed this feeling of helplessness from newcomers many times and knew Michael had had enough for his first evening at BARC.

"Let's call it a night, and we can start a new game next month when you come back," he said. "That's all I'm asking for now—that you come back. Well, and that you try to grant yourself some grace. Grace that comes with recognizing you are powerless over your kids."

"Yeah, that is one thing I do know for sure," Michael said. "They never listen to me."

"I agree. I never read in any book on raising kids that their job is to listen to their parents. Especially when they become adults, right? If you attend other meetings here, you'll likely hear people talking about their 'higher power,' however they define that. One thing I figured out early on when I was trying to fix my wife was that she had a higher power, too, and it clearly wasn't me!" They both laughed.

"Again, please give this place and these new ways of thinking a chance," Arnie continued. "I'm living proof it can help. But like most good things, it does take time and work. Speaking of work, how about a homework assignment? If you have time, it would be great if you could look over the handout on codependency from tonight. Maybe we can chat about it next month over coffee and a game? Can you help me out and promise I'll see you again?"

"Deal," Michael said.

As they corralled the chess pieces back into The Cocoon, Michael walked across the room and extracted the now furious and deflated QP from the pool of cold coffee on the floor. Fortunately, the two humans couldn't hear QP as she continued throwing the f-word around way too freely. As Michael cleaned the coffee off her felt bottom, QP thought: *Careful down there, buddy! You are really close to my special no-no place.* Indeed, she felt violated again. Sadly, this hadn't been a good first day of awareness for the little pawn.

As Michael placed the now almost-dry QP back into The Cocoon, Merlynn smelled the odor still emanating from her.

Maxwell House instant? Damn, we need to get this place a good Keurig machine.

Chapter 5

QP was exhausted after her first game of chess and the insult of having been bounced around the floor of the BARC break room. Of course, this wasn't truly her first game of chess. It was her first game after having become aware. She'd participated in thousands of games over the years; she just had no memory of them. Too tired to think about it all now, QP immediately dozed off in the warmth of the quiet, dark bottom of The Cocoon.

Merlynn was thankful that Michael and Arnie had cut their game short and that she and QP were back in The Cocoon. She recognized QP's need for rest. While QP snored, gently wedged between a bishop and another pawn, Merlynn pondered the best way to address the questions that were sure to come from her now-aware little friend when she woke. The wizard was grateful for this time to prepare. She knew the importance of planning how to address delicate issues with forethought and care rather than winging it.

The queen reflected on how many times she'd observed others handle such situations poorly by not having plans. She recalled having sat patiently on the board, listening and observing, as countless grandmasters and others practiced chess openings, the middle game, and the endgame, only to see them handle delicate and important personal matters with absolutely no endgame in mind. She had never understood this.

Unfortunately, Merlynn had observed many who failed to plan properly. However, one person came to mind who had in fact had an excellent grasp on the need for foresight and execution. He was none other than Benjamin Franklin, who, for several years, had had possession of the chess set in which she lived. After lying dormant in an antique shop for a few years in Philadelphia, Merlynn had been thrilled when this gentleman and scholar blew the dust off

The Cocoon and walked out of the cramped, musty curiosities boutique with his newly acquired chess set in hand.

Though she did question the wisdom of flying a kite in a thunderstorm, Merlynn found Mr. Franklin to be wise and insightful, for the most part, and a pretty decent chess player. Ben, as his friends called him, was one who understood the value of the game and who had shared these insights in a noted piece titled "The Morals of Chess," published in *The Columbian Magazine* in December 1786. While Mr. Franklin held the only byline to this article, Merlynn grinned with the secret that she'd played a vital role in its drafting.

This had happened late one night as John Quincy Adams, the sixth president of the United States, was visiting Franklin while the latter resided in France. They'd been engaged in an interesting game of chess and were discussing the writing of such an article when Franklin picked up Merlynn to attack President Adams's king. It was then that Merlynn had taken advantage, shooting the basic outline of "The Morals of Chess" through Franklin's hand, up his arm, and into his brilliant mind. Of course, the humble wizard permitted Mr. Franklin to take the credit.

Merlynn respected Ben's organizational skills and how he tied them into chess. Mr. Franklin often talked about the importance of knowing the impact of moving a piece, what the opponent might do to counteract the move, and how to defend from attacks. Merlynn was also fond of how Mr. Franklin focused on the big picture when playing chess and understood the need to survey the entire board as well as the relationships between different pieces depending on their positions on the board.[1]

Ben also knew the importance of having a thorough plan, as did Arnie when he helped newcomers at the recovery center. Specifically, Merlyn recalled when one of Arnie's mentees was preparing for her son to be released from inpatient treatment for methamphetamine addiction at a nearby recovery center. Arnie had encouraged the person to create an action plan for how to deal with the upcoming positive but stress-producing development.

Merlynn had sat quietly on the chess board as Arnie helped the mother put in writing her boundaries for when her son came home, how she would share these, and how she might have to change even her past way of talking with her son. Then Arnie helped his mentee roleplay what to say to her son so she had some practice with this new approach. This reminded Merlynn of another quote attributed to Mr. Franklin: "By failing to prepare, you are preparing to fail."

Another person Merlynn respected for his planning skills was President John F. Kennedy, with whom she had lived during his many years in the White House. One day, she'd heard the thirty-fifth president of the United States say to his younger brother, Bobby, while they were relaxing over a game of chess on the large wraparound porch at the family's compound in Hyannis Port, Massachusetts: "The time to repair the roof is when the sun is shining." Or—as she knew Arnie also knew well—the time to prepare for a loved one returning home from treatment was before it happened. And equally important to having a plan was practicing how to execute it.

Merlynn snapped back to the present as she heard QP stirring from her much-needed nap. For her part, QP wasted no time jumping in with questions and concerns.

"Where the hell are we? Why am I crowded between all these hard ivory things? My bottom is soggy and I smell like crappy coffee! And I can't see shit!"

Which is how Merlynn realized that, in her haste to transfer as much knowledge as possible to the little pawn in very little time, she'd forgotten to set the general context of where they were and Merlynn's role in their relationship as well as in life in general. She also realized that the inside of The Cocoon was still dark. So—thanks to her friend Ben Franklin flying the kite—Merlynn clicked on a small lamp. (Please recall: we are indulging our childlike sense of wonder and taking several leaps of faith as we proceed on this journey together. You may ask yourself, *But how did the lamp get in there? Where is the cord?* Alas, these shall remain unanswered questions.)

In the gentle beam of the lamp, Merlynn brought QP up to speed on her circumstances, where she was, and how she had just that day become aware. QP, endowed with a keen ability for critical thinking, quickly assimilated Merlynn's explanation, which satisfied many of her questions. However, the wizard's summary failed to address a key question of QP's.

"Why me and why now?" the pawn asked. "I mean, I sort of get your powers to make other pieces 'come to life,' so to speak, but why did you choose me? And why now?"

"As I am still a queen in a chess set, I know my age doesn't show," Merlynn said. "But I am very young and aging backward, as is my nature. Within a year or so, I will no longer be able to communicate with you or others. And, while this may seem egotistical—and likely is—I wanted to share my wisdom with someone else in the hope that what I have learned over the centuries may be of use to others in the future."

"Hang on a minute," QP said. "You just said you are very young but mentioned things you learned over the centuries? I don't get it."

"I understand," Merlynn responded. "I am not sure I do either. I have just learned to accept it. I have lived through the past and can see the future. I know this seems contradictory and is by any reasonable standard. But then again, I am a wizard and ask that you accept that some things in life are just unexplainable."

"Okay, I buy that you're a wizard and you have pretty cool powers, considering where we are and how we're talking like this around a bunch of inanimate objects," QP said. "But you must also be a dumbass to have picked a worthless pawn to carry on your teaching. I mean, I heard those guys say earlier that I'm only worth one stinking point!"

Okay, here we go, thought Merlynn, thankful she'd had time to organize her thoughts for what she'd known would be a difficult conversation. "Let's start with a discussion I heard a while back from grandmaster Jonathan Rowson. I think I may have mentioned him to you before—in your future—but please bear with me, as I tend to get confused about time. Aging backward as I do, I have a hard time telling the past from the present because I have lived through what you know of the present. Heck, I'm not even sure this makes any sense. I'm the one living it, and it doesn't even make sense to me.

"Anyway, back to what I recall from Mr. Rowson. I think it was after a tournament he won in Sardinia a few years back when a relative novice to the game of chess asked him his thoughts on the point values of pieces. Mr. Rowson, always willing to share his insights with anyone who took an interest in the game of chess, said something like: 'Shortly after learning how the pieces move, we are told of their relative value. Thereafter, our judgment is severely handicapped.'[2] Mr. Rowson went on to explain in more detail by talking about his view of *materialism*, a term he uses when he thinks about a chess piece's point value.

"I think—now don't quote me on this—that Mr. Rowson's main concern with point values is that each piece is so different. Each one has its own character, its own energy, and its own unique ability."

"Like my ability to get knocked on the floor and stink of coffee?" QP interrupted.

"Let's call that an unfortunate accident, not an ability," Merlynn replied. "And, even more important than ability, so much depends on a piece's position on the board and the location of other pieces around it that assigning a point value is sort of silly.[3] Although I am sure Mr. Rowson didn't use the word *silly* and phrased it much more eloquently than I did for you just now.

"And as you hang around with me more at this recovery center, you will start to see that there are many parallels between our game of chess and what people go through in their recovery. You will hear that just as each chess piece plays a unique role, so does each family member. How they interact and their positions in the family are important, just as your position is on the chess board."

Merlynn thought for a moment.

"Hey, QP, Mr. Rowson did say something specific about pawns that may help you. Something about the way pawns capture another piece by moving diagonally—that you're more valuable when you're centered. He meant the center of the board, of course, but his words seem apropos to life in general.[4] And—an interesting coincidence—we just heard Arnie and Michael talking about the importance of staying centered in the game they just played.

"My spin on staying centered is that we are stronger and more at ease with ourselves and with the situations around us when we are centered mentally. And I have found being centered involves self-confidence, or—put a bit differently—being less concerned with what other people think of our value. Which is why I agree with Mr. Rowson that the point values assigned to pieces are overblown and generally cause more harm than good.

"This also reminds me of a quote attributed to Oscar Wilde," Merlynn concluded. "'A cynic is a man who knows the price of everything but the value of nothing.'[5] QP, your value is worth more than one point to me—and to so many others!"

"What I want to know is what the price is to get out of this bag as I keep getting poked by this bishop," QP retorted.

"All good things in all good time, my little friend," Merlynn replied.

Chapter 6

As Michael drove toward BARC through the dark roads of Marietown, now bare of the holiday decorations, he reflected on the month that had passed since his first family support meeting. December had been a hard month for this single father of two, as it is for far too many people dealing with family members who are ill or no longer present. Yes, December—a month with so much pressure to be with family, a month of celebration, a month of renewal—was a brutal month for Michael.

Michael still had no idea where his son was or what his state of mind might be. And while his younger, twenty-two-year-old daughter still lived with him, their time together was hardly peaceful. They talked a little, but mostly they fought about her alcohol use. Michael attended no religious service. His home sported no decorations: no Christmas tree sparkling with ornaments, no stockings hung with care, no holiday cheer. Michael longed for them all but didn't have the energy to make any of them happen, and he felt as though going through the motions would just make him sadder. All he really wanted for Christmas was to laugh and play games with his kids like they used to. That and a good night's sleep, which continued to be an unfulfilled dream.

Though still a bit hesitant about BARC as he headed to his second meeting, he was thankful for a reason to get out of the house. Michael had taken the time to read through the handout on codependency that he'd folded up and shoved into the pocket of his grass-stained blue jeans as he left the meeting last month. He was hopeful Arnie would be there to talk about it further, and, interested in learning more about chess, he hoped for another game.

Thankfully, Goofus had consumed way too much eggnog and too many sweets over the holidays, so, still in a stupor, he didn't object as Michael pulled into the parking lot. Michael smiled as he walked by Arnie's old rusty station wagon in the same handicapped spot it had been in last month.

As Michael opened the door to BARC, he heard Brandon Artlove's voice. "Hey, welcome back! I'm glad we didn't scare you off the first time," Brandon said, upbeat as always. "It's Michael, Michael Weed, right? The Weedman! Oops, I guess that's not a good thing to yell in this place, is it?"

"Yep, good memory," Michael said. "And yeah, I have to tell my yard crews to shut up whenever they yell that nickname when we're out in public. Not really a good way to market my business." He paused. "I'm still not sure about this place, but here I am."

"All that matters for now is that you're here. Hey, I know we like some of the same music. I hope you had a chance to catch that really fun band in town from Southern California around Christmas. The Alligators? They play all Grateful Dead tunes and focus on the music of Pigpen, a former member of the Dead. And this one dude, their lead singer, wears a muumuu-type thing and hits a big gong during the songs. Really fun stuff, good tunes, and super high energy. Were you there?" As he spoke, Brandon came around the reception counter and walked with Michael down the hall toward the meeting room.

"No, sadly, I haven't seen any live music for a few years," Michael said. "Heck, I haven't done anything fun like that for as long as I can remember. All I do is work, worry about my kids, and try to sleep."

"I hear you, and I've been there, my brother. You're in the right place to start working on that—to start finding ways to have fun again. You and I are going to hit some concerts when you're ready!"

"Deal," Michael said.

With that, they reached the door to the meeting room, and Brandon headed back to the reception desk. Brandon had a wonderful knack of walking with people to their meeting rooms whenever he had the time. While he may not have realized the importance of doing so, it sent a strong message to others that they were important, worthy of someone else's time—a message many people entering BARC's doors seldom received from anyone.

Michael entered the room and took a seat in the circle right next to Arnie. As with the previous month's meeting, the ninety minutes passed very quickly. Again, the topic was codependency, and Michael learned more about it. Megan had planned on a different topic, but she started each meeting asking if anyone had questions from the previous month, and several people did. She believed it was more important to respond to the group's needs than stick to her planned discussion, so she tabled her scheduled topic until the next month.

As he listened to others around the circle share their current situations—including many challenges similar to his—Michael realized he wasn't alone on his journey. He was also pleased that Arnie again asked him for a game of chess. Gallant beamed with joy as Michael and Arnie walked toward the break room; he knew this was what his friend needed.

As Arnie untied the worn gold cord wrapped around the top of The Cocoon, QP was thankful for a breath of fresh air. It had gotten a bit stale in there over the month that had passed. She also hoped she'd stay on the board longer this game than last time, not humiliated and knocked off the table as had happened before. As it turned out, she made it halfway through the game before she was captured so was spared the embarrassment of being set aside so early. Still, she felt insignificant as she watched the other pieces move farther and with seemingly more power than she possessed.

"Did you have time for the homework assignment I gave you last time, Michael?" Arnie asked. "You know, reading the handout on codependency?"

"I actually have it right here." As Michael pulled the handout out of his pocket and unfolded it, Arnie smiled as he saw it all marked up, with some items circled in red ink. "I circled the ones I thought applied to me," Michael said. "Of the eleven items listed, I only marked six, so hey, I guess that's good, right?"

"Well, I'm glad you took so much time thinking about the handout," Arnie said. "And we aren't keeping score here, but yeah, this is one time you can be happy you didn't get one hundred percent."

Michael enjoyed how his new friend could inject subtle humor into these often depressing topics.

"I'd love to hear about the one you think is most troubling for you, the one keeping you up at night," Arnie said.

"Hard to pick just one," Michael said. "But I think 'fear of losing relationships/abandonment' and 'fear of rejection' really hit home for me. What I wanted most during the holidays was to have both my kids around. That didn't happen. My daughter, Katie, was in and out, but mostly I felt rejected by her, and I'm always scared she'll leave like my son did."

"Not that any of these are easy, but you hit two of the most challenging ones," Arnie said. "I had a hard time with those two for years with my wife. I hardly ever knew the right thing to say, and I was afraid I would drive her away." Then Arnie pointed to the one on the handout that read *problem creating and keeping boundaries.* "Sorry to jump around on the list, but I started to worry less about the fear of losing certain people in my life when I did a bunch of work on this one. I never even thought about boundaries or knew what that meant before I started coming to these meetings."

Goofus, finally shaking off the cobwebs from his holiday hangover, hated what he was hearing. "I sure wish we could ditch this old loser who keeps rattling on," the little guy screamed into Michael's ear. Gallant whispered back, encouraging Michael to stay the course.

"Once I got a better understanding of boundaries," Arnie continued, "how to set them and how to keep them—I realized some of the relationships I was so afraid of losing were not healthy ones in the first place. And a few people I was afraid might reject me ... well, sorry to sound cold, but I was probably better off without them anyway."

"I circled that one also, the one about boundaries," Michael said. "I don't even know what that means. Is it sort of like rules, or things you expect of those around you?"

"Yes, that's a good starting place to think about boundaries. This reminds me of something I heard from a chess grandmaster several years ago that can be applied to setting boundaries. And oh, by the way, that grandmaster gave me this chess set!"

"Whoa, are you a chess champion or something?" Michael said. "If you are, I'm sure glad we can't play for money here!"

"Ha, far from it!" Arnie said. "No, you see, a while back I saw a notice about a grandmaster traveling through our town, a guy named Jonathan Rowson. He was playing a chess demonstration in which he played a bunch of people at the same time."

"How the heck does that work?" Michael said. "I mean, I can't even focus on my next move in one game."

After explaining how it worked, Arnie continued with his story. "I went and played, got beaten ... if I recall right? No, I think I might have gotten a draw out of the game. Ah, that doesn't matter. What is relevant is the talk Mr. Rowson gave before the match started. I recall something he said about how he thinks in a chess game. Something about really focusing on what he is trying to achieve, what will happen next if he makes a certain move.[1]

"These questions he posed helped me start to set healthy boundaries for myself. I started to really think about what I was doing, why I was doing certain things, and what I truly wanted for myself. And the more I worked on these questions, the more I realized that how someone else will respond to what I do is not that important anymore, at least to me in my own recovery."

"Hold on," Michael said. "Your own recovery? What are you recovering from? I think you told me your wife was the one with the illness?"

"Good question. Many of the family members here refer to our own recovery in the same way addicts refer to their recovery. You see, we may not have to recover from a substance abuse issue or something like that, in the way most people think of recovery. But we do need to change our thinking. We need to move out of unhealthy patterns. We may need to change our situations. This is what I refer to when I say 'my own recovery'—that of getting healthier emotionally.

"Back to the idea of setting boundaries. As I did more work on my own recovery, I stopped thinking so much about how my wife would respond. Yes, how an opponent will respond, what move they will make next, is important in a game of chess. And, of course, sort of important when dealing with a loved one. But we can't always let how someone else will respond govern our next move."

"Dang, I worry all the time about how my kids will react to what I do," Michael said. "Sometimes I don't do what I think is best because of that fear."

"Now we are getting messy, in a good way," Arnie said. "When you focus on what you want, what you are trying to achieve, and get clarity on that, then what the other person does, how they may or may not respond, becomes less important.

"Circling back to these meetings, when I first started coming, I was here to 'fix' my wife—same as you when you said last month you were here to fix your kids. The true magic of attending these meetings and working on my own recovery happened when I started to focus on fixing myself rather than anyone else."

With this, Goofus just about lost it. The little disheveled troublemaker ran to Michael's ear and stuck his scrawny arm in as far as he could to try to cause pain and distract Michael from what Arnie was saying. He knew this conversation could reduce his power to influence Michael's thinking.

As Michael felt the pain from Goofus and from starting to realize he might need to change some well-ingrained patterns, Arnie also started talking about pain.

"I'm sensing some discomfort in your face there, Michael?" he said. "We often talk in these rooms about needing to be uncomfortable. Moving out of our comfort zones is needed most of the time for true recovery from the damage we've endured due to unhealthy relationships or childhood trauma. And back to your kids—and please understand I say this partly in jest, but there is much truth to it—if addicts or others with unhealthy habits in our lives are not mad at us, we're probably doing something wrong."

This was too much for Michael to take in all at once, so he found a nice diversion and announced with some childish satisfaction, "Speaking of doing something wrong ..." He surprised Arnie by capturing his queen, which was in the wrong place at the wrong time.

QP delighted in this as she watched Michael remove Merlynn from the board and place the wizard next to her on the table. *I guess we're even now*, QP thought.

Arnie realized that without his queen he was in a hopeless situation on the chess board, and, as the hour was getting late anyway, he tipped his king over on the board to indicate he was resigning the game. He congratulated Michael on the win.

After putting the pieces away and cleaning up a bit, he asked, "Michael, remember when Megan suggested attendees might want to attend other meetings between our monthly meetings?"

"I do. She mentioned several different meetings being held here. I think she said a good one for those with kids or friends with addiction issues was something called Nar-Anon?"

"Good memory," Arnie said. "Yep. I know you're busy despite this being a quieter time for your lawn-service business, but that meeting is next Wednesday night, and I think you might enjoy it. It's not run by a professional counselor like our meeting tonight, but I know the person who leads it, and he's pretty cool. Oh, 'cause it's me!"

They both chuckled, and Michael said he would try to make it.

Chapter 7

QP and Merlynn returned to The Cocoon after their second game of chess with Arnie and Michael. Despite still struggling with hearing she was worth only one point, she found herself smiling as she recalled Arnie moving her sideways and capturing Michael's bishop, supposedly a more powerful piece.

The experience helped her gain a better grasp on a concept Merlynn had shared earlier: a piece's position on a board determined its strength more so than its title. She also recalled how the humans had talked about that concept extending to family situations. They'd discussed how the role one chose to play in the family had a great deal of influence on one's position and strength.

Still feeling insecure about her smaller stature and, according to the point system, her lower worth than the other pieces, QP asked, "Merlynn, I know you were trying to make me feel better with all this talk about how position is more important than the material value of a piece. But I still feel crappy and less important than the others, and I want to feel better right now. If you're so powerful, cast some spell to make that happen!"

"Ah, you want immediate gratification, right?" Merlynn said. "I probably could try some spell, but you may not be happy. I may conjure up the wrong one, and who knows where you may wind up or what I might turn you into these days. And sorry, but I believe the best learning takes time and is not always easy.

"Trust that this game we are in is a great teacher, especially of patience and thinking ahead. Actually, really good players often think several moves ahead. You may have observed in the last game that Michael was quicker than Arnie to take a piece before thinking about the consequences. That is because Michael is still learning the game of chess, and he thinks more of immediate satisfaction. He tends to see taking more of Arnie's pieces as a good thing even if he puts himself in a weaker position in the long run."

"I get that," QP said. "When you made me aware, I think I recall learning something about 'winning the battle but losing the war.' Is that what happens when Michael moves too quickly?"

"Yes. Good example. We have also heard Arnie say to Michael about Michael's current situation with his kids that there is no easy fix. Unfortunately, just as there is no magic to make you feel more secure, there is no shortcut to Michael doing hard work like attending meetings and changing some of his long-established patterns."

Merlynn thought for a moment. "While I think chess is a great teacher and its lessons can be valuable in real life, there is one approach to chess I think we should not apply to our daily interactions. In chess, one goal is to resolve conflict or complexity as quickly as possible. While this may be an admirable tactic when trying to win a chess game, speed and simplicity are usually not good at unwinding human conflict. I think is was Mahatma Gandhi who said something about the need to slow down, that we shouldn't always strive to make life go faster."

Upon hearing this, QP rolled her eyes—well, she would have if she had any—as she was growing weary of Merlynn's continual name-dropping.

"While not nearly as well-known as Gandhi," Merlynn said, "another deep thinker I like and respect, Peter Block, has much to say about the problem of trying to resolve situations as fast as possible. In his insightful book *The Answer to How Is Yes*, Mr. Block warns against always trying to solve complex challenges as quickly as possible. He stresses that doing so always takes longer than we want it to. He explains:

> *The quality of our experience is not measured by the seconds on the clock, but by the timelessness of our experience. We fool ourselves if we ask how long it will take before we know who we are, become conscious, identify with our purpose, or remember our own history in a more forgiving way. The things that matter to us are measured by depth. Would you assess your humanity by its pace?*"[1]

A key point here is to try to think long-term rather than short-term," Merlynn said.

"I remember how the other day just before you were captured," QP said, "Arnie was explaining to Michael that sometimes in life, especially when making big changes to one's behavior, being uncomfortable is usually part of the process."

"Exactly. Please, QP, we have just started this journey together, and there is much to learn. Learning often requires that we move out of our comfort zones. Change is the only constant, and this often makes us and others uncomfortable. This is true of the way you're feeling right now, QP. But I know if you continue to listen, be as observant as you have been so far, and keep an open mind to the possibility of positive changes, you will start to feel better about yourself. I just can't put a time frame on how long it will take, and looking for me to create a quick fix with a chant isn't the answer. I have found over the centuries, observing and tutoring many, that a great deal of one's discomfort is linked with a strong belief that life should be a certain way. That if one does so and so, something else is guaranteed to happen. I understand this, but this type of thinking can also inhibit us from reaching our full potentials."

"I just want everything to stay the way it is. I don't like change!"

"Wanting certainty and consistency is understandable. I encourage you to remember that nothing in life is certain, though. And slowing down is often needed."

"Blah, blah, blah," QP said. "I am growing tired of your long-winded rants. I want to feel great right now. This is not helping much!"

"We really need to work on patience," Merlynn said. "I wish you had been aware when we resided with Ben Franklin, as he and I had something important to say about this in 'The Morals of Chess.' We wrote that 'we learn by chess the habit of not being discouraged by present bad appearances in the state of our affairs, the habit of hoping for a favorable change, and that of persevering in the search of resources.'"[2]

This was all too much for little QP. "I call bullshit. No way do I believe you even know Ben Franklin or these other grandmasters you keep talking about. I think you're just a confused old wizard. Stop pulling my felt-covered base!"

With this, Merlynn, who recalled the value of experiential learning, of observing something firsthand rather than just being told about it, decided it was time for a field trip.

She tried to recall the proper chant to get the two chess pieces where she wanted to take them: across the ocean to visit Ben Franklin. "FLIER, SKIER, PLIER, NILE, DIAL, OH, OLD OWL, APPEAR AND TAKE US HIGHER," chanted Merlynn from within The Cocoon. Nothing happened, and QP started to think she truly was stuck in this bag with a crazy old wizard.

"Dang it. Wrong chant," Merlynn said. "Okay, let's try this one: COCOON, BABOON, SPOON, NOON, ARCHIMEDES, PLEASE COME SOON!" Again, nothing.

And again, this was too much for QP. "We are done here, you old nut. Just make me *un*aware—or whatever term you want to use—to get rid of this so-called consciousness you say you brought me into. You're a crazy old windbag of a queen."

Merlynn continued, unabashed. "LOTION, POTION, MOTION, COMMOTION, COME MY FRIEND ARCHIMEDES AND CARRY US ACROSS THE OCEAN!"

With that, a sudden strong and cold blast of wind shot through The Cocoon, and, within a matter of seconds, QP found herself hoisted up through the snow-filled clouds into the dark sky. She felt something holding her tightly like a vise grip, firmly but not painfully. She was scared to death as she looked to her left and saw Merlynn about eight inches away from her. The wizard screamed with joy as if she were descending a steep drop on a roller coaster without a care in the world, in a state of obvious delight.

Despite the wind whipping by her at the speed of sound, QP heard Merlynn shout, "Yippee ki-yay, Archimedes, my old friend! Great to see you again after so long. Take us to our old friend Mr. Franklin, please! Preferably when he is engaged in a game of chess."

Absolutely terrified, QP looked up and saw huge wings and realized that it was a large bird just above them and that she was being held in its talons. "Well, I guess I shouldn't have doubted you, eh, Merlynn?" she said. And with that, QP passed out, either from her fear of heights or from the shock of her current situation.

Chapter 8

The time between the middle of January and the middle of February passed much more quickly for Michael than had the previous month of holiday stress. He was looking forward to the family support meeting as he pulled into BARC and was thankful see Arnie's old car next to the entrance again.

Upon entering, he received a warm greeting from Brandon Artlove, seated at the front desk as usual. As he started down the corridor toward the family support meeting, he turned abruptly and headed back toward the front entrance.

"Whoa," Brandon said. "Where are you going, pal? I hope you're not tired of getting beaten at chess by that old grump?"

"Oh, no. I started to keep a folder of handouts and other stuff I'm getting here. I left it in my car. I'll be right back."

As he approached his car, Michael passed Megan on her way in and was glad he wouldn't be late for the meeting. She also kidded him about trying to make a run for it, and he reassured her he wasn't going anywhere.

He grabbed the folder off the front seat of the car. It now contained the list of codependency traits and a few handouts he'd picked up from a table inside the room of the Nar-Anon meeting he'd attended. These other sheets included the twelve steps of Nar-Anon, some ground rules for the meeting, a list of affirmations read at the beginning of each meeting, and a list of other meetings held at locations similar to BARC.

He'd brought these tonight because he'd been looking forward to discussing them further with Arnie, hopefully over another game of chess. He was growing fonder of chess the more they played, and he'd actually started to play a little online.

Michael made it back inside BARC just as the meeting was about to start and was pleased to grab a seat next to Arnie. He loved the warm greetings and friendly nods from others he'd seen there at past meetings. He also noticed that a few people at the family support meeting had been at the Nar-Anon meeting.

Megan welcomed all, reviewed the ground rules for the meeting, and asked if anyone had questions on the topic of codependency from the previous month. Goofus jumped up and down on Michael's left shoulder with his hand in the air, hoping someone other than Michael could see and hear him as he yelled at the top of his little lungs that he had a bunch of stuff to say about this garbage. Fortunately, no one could hear him—except for Michael, that is—and Michael ignored him, which he'd been getting better at doing the more he hung around BARC. Gallant smiled, pleased with the progress Michael was making at quelling the perpetual negative self-talk of his nemesis.

As no one had further questions about codependency, Megan proceeded with her planned topic, a summary of other support meetings held at BARC and at other places around town. Michael heard more about the numerous meetings Brandon had mentioned briefly to him on his initial tour of the place and about other recovery-related meetings held nearby.

Megan encouraged all to try out other meetings to complement what they were learning and sharing at this family support meeting. She also stressed that, as many meetings were peer led, some might be more well organized than others. Unfortunately, she'd heard of a few that weren't well run, so she encouraged everyone to try different meetings until they found one that resonated with them.

After Megan completed this summary, Michael found he felt comfortable enough to share some of his personal challenges with the group for the first time. He found it freeing, especially as he felt a great deal of empathy coming from so many now-familiar faces. He briefly summarized what was going on with his daughter and son and how he was enjoying what he was learning here at BARC.

At the end of the meeting, before he again joined Arnie in a game of chess, a few people came over to Michael, introduced themselves, and shared a bit more about their experiences. One guy gave Michael his phone number and told him to call him anytime if he wanted to talk. Wow, this was a totally new experience for "The Weedman"—and he liked it!

By the time Michael made it to the break room, Arnie had already unrolled the chess board and was retrieving the chess pieces from The Cocoon.

"Ready for another whooping?" Arnie said.

"We'll have to see about that, now, won't we?" Michael said. "I've been watching videos about chess, so don't get so cocky there, buddy!"

Much to their surprise, as they set up the board, they discovered that the dark-green queen and one of the green pawns were nowhere to be found. Arnie scratched his hairless head and said this had happened before and he just didn't understand it. He said that once, he'd set up the pieces at home to do some puzzles and was positive he'd put them all back in the bag. The green queen disappeared—then, much to his amazement, she mysteriously reappeared a few days later. He wrote it off as a sign of his advancing age and failing memory, but he felt a bit concerned.

Little did either of them know that Merlynn and QP were missing because they were still with Archimedes on their field trip. Had they known this, Arnie would surely have been much more concerned about his mental health than he was about becoming a bit forgetful at his age.

"Well, no chess game tonight, I guess," Arnie said. "You lucked out. Want to head home?"

"Oh, no, I really wanted to talk more about what you and others shared at the Nar-Anon meeting. That is, if you have time?"

"You bet. I'm grateful you showed up for that meeting." With this, Michael reached for his folder and took out the handouts from the Nar-Anon meeting.

Arnie smiled, noticing that Michael had made notes on these just as he had with the other handouts. "You are taking this stuff seriously, I see."

"Trying to. Okay, honestly though, I can't get past the first one on this twelve-step Nar-Anon list that says I have to admit I am powerless over the addict. Yeah, I'm down with the second line that says my life is unmanageable—heck, isn't everyone's life out of control? But if I have no power over my kids, why am I even here? I mean, am I supposed to just give up?"

Arnie empathized with the pain he felt emanating from Michael, and he fully understood the emotions. He'd helped many others process similar reactions to Step One. He responded using a communication technique he'd learned at BARC many years earlier referred to as SET, standing for support, empathy, and truth.

"First, Michael, I hear you loud and clear, feel your pain, and fully understand this question. You're not alone in feeling this way. I had the exact same questions and doubts about Step One several years ago, as do many when they start down this road.

"The truth is, though—or let me say the truth I have come to accept—we are truly powerless over anyone else if we think about it. And while I know this can sound defeatist, I find it actually freeing. Freeing in that this acceptance brings me peace of mind and restores some manageability, if that's even a word, to my life."

"Yeah, but … so I do nothing about my kids?"

"Ah, again, we are getting messy in a good way. No, just the opposite. You being here, while it has to be primarily for yourself—for your own health and peace of mind—can do more for your kids than anything else I know of. The healthier you get, the better the chance your kids will see this and maybe, just maybe, get into recovery themselves. But that shouldn't be the reason you do the work here. You need to do it for yourself.

"Okay, sorry, but here I go with another chess quote," Arnie said. "A famous grandmaster, Viswanathan Anand, once said, 'Once you understand that you are lost, you can do anything.'[1] While he meant the way this thought freed him up in a game of chess, I think the same applies to life in general. It reminds me that once I truly accept the only things I have control over are my own actions and thoughts, I become free."

"Wow. I sort of get it," Michael said. "Sorry, but it may take me a while to fully embrace this way of thinking."

"As it should. This isn't easy stuff, nor is your situation. Do you have any other questions?"

"I hope you don't lose respect for me over this, but I'm not religious," Michael said. "I mean, I'm not critical of those who are or anything like that. It's just that I don't really buy into the whole idea of a God who actively responds to prayers or stuff like that. Oh man, I don't even like talking about religion. I hope I haven't offended you. The whole idea of turning things over to some higher power doesn't feel authentic for me."

"Not offended at all. I truly appreciate your honesty. And I like how comfortable you must be with our friendship that you can be vulnerable enough to broach the topic of religion with me. Trust me, while I do believe in a higher power, I'm humble enough to respect other opinions. I think a big problem with religion—no, not with religion, but with some people who claim to be religious—is that when people are so convinced they have all the answers, they judge others harshly. Not sure that was anyone's intended message with religion."

"I have all the answers," Goofus said, "if you would just listen to me more! Higher power my foot. Come on, let's ditch this place!"

Fortunately, Michael was learning to quiet Goofus much more quickly than he had before he started coming to BARC.

"But I'm getting off topic here," Arnie continued. "Back to your concern. Yes, this is a common concern some have with twelve-step approaches. A couple of thoughts may help. As you don't see yourself as religious in a traditional sense, maybe you can think more about the higher power as a reference to your internal thinking? Work on identifying the 'power greater than ourselves' as what's going on in your own head."

"That makes sense," Michael responded. "Or, how about thinking of the power of the meeting, the force of what we learn together here as a 'higher power'?"

"Perfect way to phrase this! And if the spiritual aspect of this approach is truly a stumbling block for you, there are other options. One is referred to as the SMART Recovery process. I'm not that familiar with it—I'm not even sure what the initials stand for—but I don't think it places as much emphasis on a higher power. There are SMART-based meetings on the list you have there, and I think Megan handed out a summary of the SMART approach at the meeting earlier. You could always check those out. I would hate for you to be turned off and stop this new journey of yours if the twelve steps don't work for you."

"Ha ... smart recovery would leave him out," Goofus said to Arnie, who could not hear him, thank goodness.

"I also think there's some twelve-step stuff for agnostics or atheists. Let's Google it to see what we can find." Arnie walked over and pulled up a search engine on one of BARC's open computers. "Okay, look, here's a twelve-step list for agnostics. It looks to me like the major change is that they replace references to a higher power with phrases like 'collective wisdom' and 'accepting strength beyond our awareness.' Maybe reviewing this will be helpful."

"I like this list a lot," Michael said. "To be clear, I do like some of the other ideas in the twelve steps, like making amends to people I may have harmed or taking an inventory of myself. I've become a pretty good list maker with my business, too, and I can get down with those ideas. I may work on those before our next game."

With this, Goofus launched a plan to hide all pens and paper around the house to prevent Michael from following through, while Gallant made a mental note to hide some pens from Goofus.

Chapter 9

As Archimedes continued his flight through the night sky, Merlynn looked forward to reuniting with Ben Franklin and hoped the still-passed-out QP would benefit from this visit as well.

QP came to just as the wise old owl flew through an open window, perched carefully on an ornate metal chandelier, and placed his passengers safely on an arm of the fixture. The pawn had tons of questions about how they had gotten here and why but, still in a state of shock, held her tongue for a bit.

Merlynn, pleased to look down and see two people sitting on opposite sides of a chess board, at first assumed she had conjured up the right spell. Upon further inspection, she realized something just wasn't right. The first clue that something was amiss: apparently, Mr. Franklin had lost a huge amount of weight and grown several inches taller than Merlynn remembered. Also, his hair, which had been prematurely white and thinning, was now coal-black and thick.

Merlynn's puzzle was solved when she heard from below, "It is your move, Mr. Lincoln." While pleased to see another old friend, Abe Lincoln, with whom she had lived in the White House for a few years, the wizard could not understand how her chant could have landed them so far off. This second mystery was solved when Merlynn glanced over her shoulder at Archimedes and saw that mischievous "I know better than you" grin under his large, protruding beak.

"Okay, what's going on here?" Merlynn asked the owl. "We were supposed to be with Ben Franklin, not Lincoln! Have you gone daft?" She was thankful that Lincoln, who she knew was soon to be President Lincoln at this time, and his playing partner, who turned out to be Judge Samuel H. Treat, Chief Justice of the Illinois Supreme Court, could not hear them.

"Yes, I know this isn't Mr. Franklin, and, no, I am as smart and cunning as always," Archimedes said. "More so than you are, I might note. And you didn't screw up the chant, for a change. I just thought your impatient little pawn could benefit from what is about to happen below us, so we flew to Springfield instead."

QP was about to object to the owl's not-so-kind characterization of her when a little boy entered the room below them.

"Dad," said eight-year-old Todd Lincoln, "Mother said you are to come home right away."

"Go tell Mother I will be home soon," Mr. Lincoln said.

Satisfied, little Todd left the stately room.

As the game below continued, QP came out of her daze and said, "What the heck was going on, and what was up with the giant bird sitting next to them?"

"This is Archimedes," said Merlynn. "He has been with me for centuries. He has the power to take us wherever we want to go—and sometimes to places we don't want to go!"

Suddenly, Todd appeared once again with a now more urgent message from Mrs. Lincoln that Abe was to come home immediately. Abe, being an avid chess player and not one to end a game until its conclusion, once again informed Todd to tell his spouse he would be home shortly.

With this, much to everyone's surprise, Todd reached out and kicked the chess table so hard the pieces flew all over the place. Stunned, Judge Treat—and those surreptitiously perched above him—expected a harsh reaction from Mr. Lincoln to this act of insolence. They were all surprised at Mr. Lincoln's response.

"Well, Judge, I guess that is Todd's game! You set 'em up again and we will have it out some other day. Come along, Todd. Let us go see what Ma wants." And, without other words, he took the boy by the hand and strode calmly away.[1]

"And there you have it," Archimedes said. "*That* is exactly why we came here rather than to Mr. Franklin. Listen up, QP. I have been observing you since you became aware a few months ago. And, while you have learned much, despite being with her"—he pointed his wing toward Merlynn and rolled his big owl eyes—"I thought you needed a lesson in patience and in controlling your emotions. Mr. Lincoln could have reacted harshly to what Todd did. Instead, he kept his cool and just moved on. My takeaway is that, regardless of what happens, we always have a choice in how we respond, and exercising restraint and patience is usually the best course of action."

"I am still not pleased you took us somewhere other than my chant directed, Archimedes," Merlynn said. "But, yes, this is a good lesson for all of us. And, as usual, this reminds me of something I read many years ago—or in the future, maybe? In his book *Secrets of Grandmaster Chess*, John Nunn wrote about how patience can be the attacker's greatest asset when the opponent has no counterplay.[2]

"Now, to be clear, in this case, we need to think of our 'opponents' as ourselves—our own self-talk, what goes on in our heads—rather than something someone else may be contemplating. While developing a plan that looks several steps ahead may take more time than a quick attack, it is usually better to take more time, exercise patience, and avoid the immediate gratification sometimes obtained by a quick move, as this results in a better outcome most of the time."

Archimedes chimed in. "Another thing chess players need to remember is that every pawn can become a queen."

QP would have grown flushed if her green ivory had allowed it. "What? I am just a pawn. I am only worth *one point*! How can I become a queen?"

Archimedes continued, "I am surprised … no … *not* surprised that this old queen has not explained this yet! You see, QP, if you make it all the way to the other side of the board, the person who moved you there has a choice to turn you into any other piece on the board, except for the king. And, usually, but not always, they will opt to turn you into a queen. They can do so even if their queen is still on the board, so there can be two queens of the same color on the board at the same time—even more than two if the player advances additional pawns to the other side of the board."

"Wow, this is pretty cool," QP said.

"Please permit me to build on Archimedes' statement that every pawn can be transformed into a different piece," the wizard said. "Players often forget the true power of a pawn until much later in the game. Chess players and others need to think long-term rather than short-term to help them make better decisions."

"Hey, Merlynn," Archimedes said. "My wings are starting to freeze up, and I am getting bored here. I am ready to take flight from this old, musty place. I think your student could benefit from another story about the importance of patience and playing the long game. Do we have time for another trip?"

"Always time for you. What do you have in mind?"

"Let's go visit that friend of yours, Eugene Brown, at his Big Chair Chess Club in Washington, DC."

"Ah, Eugene! Great idea, Archimedes. I haven't seen him since he was incarcerated, but I have followed his moving story. Shall I conjure up a spell to get us there?"

"Oh, please don't!" the wise owl cried. "I trust my instincts better on this one than I trust your ancient memory!" With that, Archimedes grabbed QP and Merlynn in his talons and flew through the same window they had entered a half hour earlier. They left Judge Treat picking up scattered chess pieces, still in awe at the restraint and patience shown by Mr. Lincoln.

Their journey back to the present was a quick and uneventful one, and they soon arrived at their destination: Eugene Brown's Big Chair Chess Club. Their timing was fortuitous, as Mr. Brown was speaking with a group of visitors about his history, about how learning to play chess in prison had transformed his life, and about the mission of the Big Chair Chess Club.

After sharing the details about his troubled youth and time in prison for robbing a bank, Mr. Brown said this, "There are three phases to a chess game: the opening, the middle, and the end, and you have to put them all together to win. You just don't win in the opening. That is what I was trying to do when I robbed that bank. I was trying to win in the opening. I was trying to get instant results. If you keep making bad moves in chess, you are going to get checkmated. On the street, it isn't checkmate, it's your life. It's a wheelchair. It's incarceration."[3]

The founder of this remarkable chess center then stated the mission of the Big Chair Chess Club: "to teach the un-teachable, reach the un-reachable, and help others discover the power that comes from always thinking before they move."[4] He explained that his goal was to teach inner-city children and adults how chess can help in life by improving one's concentration and self-discipline.

QP was stunned. What she'd thought until now was just a kid's game had such power. The power to transform lives. She also saw the tie-ins to her newfound understanding of patience from the lesson learned from Abe Lincoln—and that she could become anything if she kept moving ahead and made it to the endgame. Her confidence was growing move by move, lesson by lesson.

Chapter 10

While Michael's landscaping business started to pick up as the weather warmed mid-March, he still found time to attend the family support meeting at BARC.

On this evening, the topic was communication strategies and managing expectations. Megan approached it by first breaking down the Serenity Prayer. Michael had read it several times while at BARC, as it was posted in every meeting room. Though familiar with it, he appreciated Megan's more in-depth, line-by-line review of the prayer and ways to actually put it into practice.

First, Megan read the Serenity Prayer:

God, grant me the serenity to accept the things I cannot change,
The courage to change the things I can,
And the wisdom to know the difference.

Then she began by talking about the first line: finding serenity and a way to accept things one could not change. With respect to serenity, she used a word Michael was not familiar with: *equanimity*. Megan defined it as the ability to stay calm and composed even in chaotic situations. She offered helpful tools to accomplish this, such as meditating, taking a deep breath before acting, talking to a friend or sponsor, and not taking oneself so seriously all the time.

An attendee raised his hand and asked to speak.

"Of course," responded Megan.

"Thank you," the man said. "A friend once told me, along these same lines, that my challenge was to find a way to accept the unacceptable. Does that apply here?"

"Absolutely," Megan responded. "This is a powerful statement and a good way to look at it."

This phrase really resonated with Michael, and he wrote it in his always present notebook with a reminder to make a sticky note to place on his dashboard.

Megan moved on to the second line: the courage to change the things one could. She said it took courage to change previous patterns, step out of comfort zones, and try new things, even if—or especially if—they felt foreign. She noted something Michael had heard previously from Arnie: that if something felt comfortable to someone in the throes of codependency, that was often a sign that it was the wrong thing to do.

When she came to the last line—the wisdom to know the difference—Megan said that the best way to accomplish this wisdom was to stay involved in a supportive environment like BARC and continue on a journey of becoming an aware, lifelong learner. Michael found himself nodding, as he did feel he'd changed and learned a great deal the past four months. He'd actually started to set some boundaries with his daughter at home and wasn't worrying so much about his son, who was still missing.

The discussion then turned to various ways to communicate with someone in active addiction or with some other form of mental illness. Megan began by warning about getting into a debate with someone in active addiction, as it was often futile and useless. She shared something she'd heard from another therapist a while back, who had made an analogy (admittedly, a somewhat crude one): "You wouldn't walk into your backyard and intentionally step in dog shit, would you? Entering into a debate with someone in active addiction is the same, a truly no-win situation." Another way of saying this, Megan said, was that arguing with someone in active addiction was like trying to blow out a lightbulb.

Megan then moved on to a more concrete example of a communication strategy referred to as SET—standing for support, empathy, and truth. In this approach, the "support" part started with an "I" statement intended to establish a nonthreatening foundation for more dialogue. It demonstrated that the speaker cared and truly heard what the other person was saying. For example, "I care about you."

The "empathy" part shifted to feelings and was intended to let the other person know that the speaker understood how they felt. Megan explained how acknowledging emotions may be useful: for example, by saying, "I see you are angry" or "I understand why you are upset, as I know other parents deal with this differently."

Finally, Megan discussed how "truth" should focus on an honest assessment of the circumstances as the speaker saw them. For example, "This is what I can do" was a truth statement. Another phrase some found worked well as a truth statement was, "This isn't working for my recovery." The beauty of truth statements was that they shifted the discussion away from whatever the addict may want and put the emphasis back on the needs of the codependent person. Making a statement about one's own truth changed the focus of the dialogue. Megan stressed that one might have to just keep repeating the truth statement to avoid getting pulled back into a dialogue with someone in active addiction.

***

Michael was quieter than usual after the meeting. Arnie sensed something was troubling him. "You okay? Pretty quiet there ... and that is one furrowed brow."

"Dang, is it that obvious?" Michael said. "It's hard to explain. I just feel overwhelmed with all this new stuff I'm hearing. I sort of get that I need to change some ways I've been dealing with my kids and even the way I've been thinking about them. I just don't know what the right thing to do is. It makes me want to do nothing, sort of like being afraid to even make the next move on this chess board."

"Your feelings are not uncommon for someone learning more about recovering from codependency and dealing with losses," Arnie said. "And there is a term for this. It's 'the paralysis of analysis.'"

"Yeah, I do feel sort of stuck or frozen right now," Michael said. "And somehow I have a feeling you'll find a way to tie this to the game of chess?"

"You know me all too well," Arnie said. "The link to chess is pretty straightforward. Bobby Fischer—a player you may have heard of from his famous world championship match against Boris Spassky in 1972—said it best. He said something like, 'Don't worry about finding the best move. Seek always to find a good move.'[1] Another saying often quoted by grandmasters is, 'If you can't find a good move, don't play a bad one.'"[2]

He continued. "Other chess players often talk about being bold—not reckless, but not timid either. Now, I should emphasize that you should only be bold after considering all the options, after thorough reflection, after thinking about the move you want to make after this one. And, once you decide, avoid the 'shoulda, woulda, coulda' trap of hindsight."

"Ah, I think I get it," Michael said. "We never truly know the outcomes of our actions. It's often trial and error. Sometimes we are right and sometimes we are wrong. And it is through this that we learn. Am I close?"

"Exactly. This reminds me of the ancient parable of the Taoist farmer I heard many years ago, one I try to carry with me. The gist of it is that neighbors observe what they consider to be good and bad things happening to the farmer. When they tell the farmer they think something good happened, the farmer responds, 'Maybe good, maybe bad.' Likewise, when his neighbors say they think something bad happened, he responds, 'Maybe bad, maybe good.' In the end, one comes to realize something that appears negative initially may actually turn out to be a blessing, and vice versa."

"That's a great story," Michael said. "I need to keep that in mind in my lawn-service business as well. I often get stuck worrying whether we are doing the right thing for a client, whether they'll be happy with what we did after we are done.

"And another friend of mine said something just the other day sort of like this story. We were talking about how we had met about two years ago. He had just purchased a new house and hadn't even moved to town yet when a neighbor noticed a major leak in his irrigation system. Fortunately for both of us, he called me after Googling landscapers with good ratings. I fixed his leak, and we've become good friends because of that. So this leak in his yard, which wasn't good at the time, resulted in our friendship. I guess it's all about how we look at things, right?"

"Perfect example!" Arnie said. "This highlights that we really do have a choice in how we look at any situation. Sort of a 'Do you see the glass as half-full or half-empty?' deal. And if we have a choice, why not opt for looking for the positive in the situation? Or, at least, let's not assume there's nothing good to learn from it. I've found some of my best learning comes from difficult situations."

"Yeah, but I still struggle with having to make a decision when there are several choices," Michael said. "I feel stuck at times, especially with choices about how to act with my kids."

"This isn't always easy. After considering options, sometimes we have to make what we think is the best move. Even if we aren't sure of the outcome, there comes a time when we have to make a move and trust our gut instincts."

"There is one thing you haven't mentioned yet, Arnie. To show I was listening at the Nar-Anon meeting you led the other week, what about contacting your sponsor or a trusted friend before making a hard decision?"

"Wow, the student has become the teacher. I sensed some hesitancy in all that talk about getting a sponsor, Michael. Are you on board with that?"

"Thinking about it. I get the need for insight from others, especially those who have been on this journey longer than my four months. I know I benefit from talking with you and others I've met here, but, no, I haven't attempted to find a sponsor yet."

Chapter 11

Archimedes flew silently through the clear March night, returning his passengers to The Cocoon for a well-needed rest. While pleased with his decision to defy Merlynn's directive to visit Mr. Franklin, he hoped they would visit him again, as he also cherished the time they spent with him.

Upon approaching Marietown, Merlynn awoke and had a premonition: a discussion about to take place between Michael and his daughter, Katie. He asked Archimedes to take a detour to Michael's home so QP could observe this interaction.

Archimedes flew carefully down Michael's chimney with Merlynn and QP still on his back and perched on the fireplace mantel. QP was not happy at all about being covered in the black, tar-like creosote that caked the sides of the old brick chimney. She quickly forget how dirty she was as she heard Michael's voice from below them.

"I just can't have you drinking in my home any longer, nor coming in here drunk," Michael said to his daughter.

"I can't believe this!" Katie said. "So are you going to kick me out of my own home? Where would I go? How would I survive? A bunch of my friends are still living at home, and *their* parents don't care what they do! This isn't fair."

Practicing the SET principles, Michael said, "I hear you, and I understand that other parents do things differently. And I know this is a change for you and for me. I'm doing this because I care about you. I also can appreciate why you feel as though this is not fair. I can tell you are frustrated. The truth is, your drinking here and being around me when you're drunk is not working for my recovery. And no, I am not kicking you out of our home. I am setting a boundary. If you choose to not follow it, you are making the choice to leave."

After a bit more back and forth, Katie screamed, "Total bullshit! I see why my brother left! Okay, I'm out of here." The door slammed so hard behind Katie, all were surprised the glass panels didn't shatter.

Michael sat on the couch, head in his hands, and wept. Feeling somewhat guilty about observing this very personal interaction, the three voyeurs quietly took their leave.

Upon returning to The Cocoon, Archimedes decided to join his friends for a while despite the inconvenience of having to make himself the size of a hummingbird to do so.

Once settled in, QP surprised the other two with the following statement: "You know, seeing how I can capture other pieces, and understanding my importance in chess—especially in the endgame, when I can become a queen or any other piece—I think I have learned enough. I appreciate everything you've taught me, but I don't think I need any more lessons."

"While I am glad you are feeling better about yourself, I trust you can handle my bluntness," Merlynn said. "That comment proves one thing. Do you want to know what it proves?"

"Um, given your tone, I doubt it."

"Well, I am telling you anyway."

"Yeah, I was afraid of that."

"It is great that you are feeling more confident. But thinking you have learned all you need to know is extremely dangerous. I think it is time for a lesson on the drawbacks of complacency. This is sort of a 'both/and' situation. On one hand, it is great to feel comfortable with where you are, with your opinion of yourself, and with what is going on with those around you. All good. The negative comes when we think we are done learning. It is so very easy to get lazy with that kind of attitude and to slip back into negative patterns. Stories from three books come to mind here."

"Can we keep it to one or two please?" the newly self-assured pawn said.

"We will see. The first story that comes to mind is from prolific British author and winner of the Nobel Prize in Literature, Doris Lessing. One of her books, *The Marriages Between Zones Three, Four, and Five*, contains a great parable about complacency. In short, it is a sci-fi love story in which people live in different zones. Zone Four is a very hostile place where the residents spend their entire lives protecting their borders from imaginary predators. Zone Three, on the other hand, is a very loving, peaceful place high in the mountains above Zone Four. Here the residents spend all their time and energy on the arts, humanities, and other intellectually stimulating activities."

"Like playing chess?" QP asked.

"I don't recall Ms. Lessing writing about them playing chess, but, yes, similar activities. As the story unfolds, we learn that the people in Zone Four have a law that prohibits them from looking up at the blue, misty mountains of Zone Three. If someone gets caught doing so, then, as punishment, they have to wear a very heavy metal helmet that prevents them from lifting their head so they cannot gaze up at the peaks. When the queen of Zone Three learned of this, she was appalled at how terrible and barbaric the rule seemed to her.

"Then, something even more troubling dawned on her. She realized that because of their complacency, her people, the residents of Zone Three, never bothered to look up at the even more mystical purple and pink peaks of Zone Two. There was no law against doing so, no punishment if they ventured there, no mandated heavy helmet; they just never looked farther than their own horizons because they were so comfortable and content. Suddenly she felt sorrier for her people than she did for those in Zone Four.[1]

"Again, there is nothing wrong with being satisfied with one's condition or place in life, as long as that contentment does not prevent further growth."

Merlynn paused to make sure her student was still paying attention. She was pleased to see QP fully awake and apparently contemplating the moral of the story she just shared.

"The second story, from another favorite book of mine, highlights the importance of being a lifelong learner. It's a book from a relatively unknown author, which is unfortunate, as it contains wonderful words of wisdom. It was written by a very intelligent, insightful, and stunningly handsome man named Lance Wilson, whom I hope you have the pleasure of meeting someday. The book is titled *Dashboard Bagels: Dishing Up Food for Thought*. In one chapter, Mr. Wilson tells of an early mentor of his, a brilliant jurist, who said he hoped to die the most ignorant man who ever lived. The ever-curious Mr. Wilson found this puzzling, so he asked his mentor about his seemingly odd statement. His mentor explained that every time he learned something new—which he tried to do every day—he realized just how much he didn't know and how much more there was to learn. Thus, the potential that comes with seeing one's ignorance. I consider the jurist a great example of a true lifelong learner."

"The third book this lesson calls to mind, Garry Kasparov's *How Life Imitates Chess*, brings us back to the game of chess. Kasparov talks about the need to try new things to avoid resting on our laurels."

"What are 'laurels'?" QP asked.

"They are a type of shrub."

"Well, why wouldn't you want to rest on them? Are they thorny?"

"Ah, I see. You are curious about where this term originated. I am glad to see you still want to learn," Merlynn said with a grin. "The term goes back to ancient Greece, when wreaths made of laurel leaves were given to athletes who won events."

"Now that makes sense," QP said.

"Good. So Mr. Kasparov said we need to continually expand our horizons to avoid becoming complacent."[2]

"Okay, I get it!" QP said. "I'm sure there is still more I can learn. So can we go on another fun field trip if you think you can get the right chant this time?"

"Point of clarification: I had the right chant. That owl defied me again."

"Yes, I did," Archimedes replied. "And, we learned a good lesson, right?"

"Good point," Merlynn responded. "I am glad you agree there is more to learn, QP. As for another field trip, we had better put that on hold while Arnie is still looking around his house for us. We should stay here to ease his concern. Actually, it would have been better if Archimedes had left us somewhere Arnie could find us so we wouldn't mysteriously appear back in The Cocoon. But that is an easy chant I know I can get right. I will place us under the couch, right at the edge where he can clearly see us."

"It had better be clean there!" QP quipped.

"Let's find out. OH, GRAND MAGIC OF MOVEMENT, GET US OUT OF THIS POUCH AND PLACE US UNDER THE COUCH!" *Poof!* With that correct incantation, QP and Merlynn found themselves on Arnie's hardwood floor under the very front of his couch where they could easily be seen. QP was impressed Merlynn has gotten it right and pleased it seemed clean in their new resting place. Then her pleasure quickly changed to disdain as she noticed a dead ant right next to her.

"Dead ant, dead ant, dead ant!"

At first Merlynn envisioned a pink panther from one of her favorite cartoons—until she noticed the actual dead ant next to them. Looking back a bit, the queen observed a string of ants marching dutifully toward their designated destination. "Well, hello, old friends. I haven't seen ants for a very long time. Not since I taught King Arthur a valuable lesson when I turned him into one. Maybe that should be your next field trip. Want to become an ant and join them while we wait for Arnie to find us?"

"Hell no!" QP said. "Don't even think about it. What can you learn from ants about anything?"

"Tons. In fact, one lesson ties nicely into the complacency we have been talking about. Just because something is little doesn't mean we can't learn much from it. Actually, this is sort of a 'both/and' story as well. Ants are extremely proficient, actually—one of the most efficient species that exists. They perfected how to survive and thrive millions of years ago, even way before I came into existence."

"Hard to believe anything is older than you!"

"Very funny. May I proceed uninterrupted?"

"If you must."

"Why, thank you! Being proficient is good in many ways, of course. However, an extreme level of proficiency can, unfortunately, bring with it complacency. Ants stopped evolving eons ago. As Arthur learned when he lived among them, their language is very limited as well. Ants' vocabulary consists mainly of two words, meaning *done* and *not done*. Ants who are doing what they are supposed to be doing and following the rules are 'done.' Those who fall out of line, get injured, or do anything out of the ordinary are 'not done' and wind up getting executed."[3]

"I am glad I am not an ant," QP said. "And I get the need to continue to learn to keep growing. Sorry I was so rude earlier."

"No worries," Merlynn responded. "We have seen firsthand how Michael is benefiting from stepping out of familiar patterns, from trying different approaches to how he thinks about his kids' challenges. What was your takeaway from the discussion we saw between Michael and his daughter, Katie?"

"Well, she was really pissed off when Michael made it clear she could no longer drink in his home," QP said. "I loved how Michael stood his ground, didn't react, and didn't waiver. He didn't even raise his voice. He followed the support, empathy, and truth approach he had learned, and it seemed to work. Especially when he stated his 'truth' that her drinking in his home was not working for his recovery."

"You listened well, QP. Great observations. We both know that was not an easy discussion for him. But yes, he held his ground, stayed unemotional, and followed what he had practiced. One of my favorite parts was when she yelled at him that he had been brainwashed at BARC, and he said, 'Well, maybe my brain needed washing.' It is sad she opted to leave, though, rather than abiding by his new boundary. But that was her choice."

"Yep, I'm sure he's worried about where she is and if she's okay. And he handled it well when she accused him of kicking his own child out of her home. He calmly reminded her he wasn't kicking her out and that it was her choice to leave if she could not abide by the boundary he had set."

"Well said, QP, well said. This reminds me of something I heard from a grandmaster a while back ..."

QP was about to object to this ongoing lecture from Merlynn when she was rescued upon hearing from above, "Well, dang, there you two are, right under the couch. How the heck did I miss you when I looked there before? I'd better get these glasses checked." With that, Arnie reached down and retrieved the two wandering chess pieces and looked even more perplexed to feel them covered with soot.

"What the hell? How the heck did you two get so dirty just lying there?" Upon wiping them down thoroughly, Arnie returned QP and Merlynn to The Cocoon. The chess pieces were exhausted from their travels and thankful for this time to rest up before their next game.

Chapter 12

Michael pulled his Weed No More truck into the driveway of his home just in time to catch a shower and head to BARC for the April family support meeting. While he now had three crews working and had spent twelve hours at different job sites, he wasn't about to miss the special guest speaker tonight.

Megan had announced last month that Dr. Mel Pohl would be speaking about the brain disease of addiction. Michael was very interested in this topic, as he had to admit he was still resistant to the idea that drinking and using drugs was an actual disease. He just didn't understand why people couldn't stop if they really wanted to.

Michael was also glad to have a reason to get out of the house, which had felt so empty since Katie stormed out a few weeks ago. While his house was a bit too quiet for him and he was having doubts about the boundaries he'd set, there was much less drama. He felt pretty darn good about the calmness. He'd actually gotten a decent night's sleep last night as well—a first in a very long time.

Michael entered the meeting and took a seat right next to Arnie as Megan introduced Dr. Pohl. Megan noted that Dr. Pohl was currently the senior medical consultant to the Pain Recovery Program at The Pointe Malibu Recovery Center and formerly the chief medical officer for the Las Vegas Recovery Center. She reviewed his many credentials and noted the several books he'd authored on treating the underlying causes of chronic pain. Megan then distributed a copy of an article Dr. Pohl had written for the State Bar of Nevada, titled "The Brain Disease of Addition," which the doctor referenced during his talk.[1]

Dr. Pohl began by sharing, "An addict's brain is struggling against animalistic urges to use its drug of choice that's on par with the need to eat and sleep. It's a disease that doesn't rest in the more reason-based frontal lobe but in the dopamine-laden and rewired 'rat brain' that says, get me that drug now."[2]

He went on to share a story of one of his clients, a young woman identified as Cindy, who suffered from heroin addiction. She had already been arrested and admitted into drug court and faced its rigid schedule of drug testing. Cindy knew she would be going to jail if she tested positive one morning, yet she used heroin before the test. "So, that's what we're dealing with, and it's pretty powerful stuff," he said.[3]

Michael raised his hand and asked, "Dr. Pohl, please help me understand how addiction is an illness. I still don't get that part of it."

"Thank you for the question," Dr. Pohl responded. "Addiction is clearly a chronic, progressive, and potentially fatal brain disease. The brain is composed of countless cells and controls all of our actions. It is divided into several parts. The most relevant one for today's discussion is the midbrain, often referred to as the reptile brain. This governs our survival functions and emotions and is the part which can often drive addictions."[4]

While Gallant, Michael's better angel, usually took the high road and avoided cheap insults like the ones his counterpart Goofus launched regularly, at times even he could not resist.

"Hey, Michael," Gallant whispered into his ear. "Reptile brain is sitting on your other shoulder right over there! Oh, sorry, I shouldn't insult all reptiles like that."

Michael couldn't suppress a soft chuckle at this quip as Goofus strained around his neck trying to figure out what was so funny.

Dr. Pohl continued, "The addicted brain causes the person to continue to use even though they no longer get the original 'high' and not stop even when bad things start to happen due to their usage. The drug works so well it develops survival salience, which means that the person's brain thinks and feels like it needs the drug to survive—even more than food, water, sleep, or sex. This state results in the pathological pursuit of reward and/or relief."[5]

As he knew he was speaking to family members who were dealing with loved ones with substance abuse issues, Dr. Pohl concluded his remarks by stressing how important their continued involvement in meetings like this was for their own recovery and well-being. He reiterated that the disease of addiction would certainly kill the addicted person if left unchecked and that it also had the power to kill loved ones if they took no action to heal from the trauma. He closed by saying how impressed he was that so many people were taking the time to attend these meetings at BARC and encouraged them to keep coming back.

***

Following an informative question-and-answer period, Michael and Arnie made their way to the break room for their regular monthly game of chess and banter. As they set up the board, Brandon accompanied Dr. Pohl into the room, as he'd asked for a cup of coffee before heading back to his hotel.

"Dr. Pohl, I am pleased to introduce you to two of our valued friends here at BARC, Arnie Zugzwang and Michael Weed."

Dr. Pohl paused, rubbed his bearded chin, and, with a sly grin, said, "Artlove, Weed, and Zugzwang, now that's three interesting last names. And, hey"—he shifted his gaze toward Michael— "so, we had Weed in our meeting tonight? That's not cool." He turned toward Arnie. "Zugzwang, and you play chess? I have dabbled in the game a bit and know the definition of *zugzwang* when linked to a game of chess. But I have never heard it as a person's name."

"First, it's great meeting you, and I enjoyed your talk tonight," Arnie said. "I heard about the place you previously worked, the Las Vegas Recovery Center. I had a friend who attended the four-day family-renewal program they offered, and she loved it. She said she learned a great deal from you and others about family structures, how the brain works, and various coping mechanisms."

"Well, thank you. Unfortunately, the Las Vegas Recovery Center closed a couple of years ago, but, yes, we place a great emphasis on family involvement in the recovery process. Just like you all do here at BARC. Now, what's up with your last name?"

"Well, it's an interesting story," Arnie said. "As the legend goes—I have no idea if it's true or not—my great-great-grandfather took on this rather strange name, sort of proving what I've heard about him being an eccentric, maybe even a little crazy. He was an avid chess player in Germany in the early 1800s. As my grandfather told me, his dad often got into helpless positions when playing chess, so he combined two German words to make this name. You see, *zug* in German means 'move' and *zwang* means 'compulsion.' So, put together, as it applies to chess, it has come to mean being forced to make a move that only makes your position worse. This usually happens in the endgame. Now, why he would want a name like that, and decided to stick his future generations with it, is beyond me. He must have been a bit mad."

"That's fascinating," Dr. Pohl said. "And it does line up with my understanding of the term as it applies to chess. I have often thought that the interpretation is a strange twist of semantics and could easily be turned into something more positive. I have thought about this in recovery as well. I mean, yes, in some sense, I can understand how needing to make a move may seem to only worsen one's position, in chess and in life. But, taking a glass-half-full approach, if it is still the best move you have, albeit a seemingly bad one, then isn't it really the best option? Sorry if this is pretty abstract, but I would rather look for the best outcome than consider something a lost position. Sure, sometimes things get worse before they get better, but doing nothing is not usually a good option either."

"I love that different outlook on my last name," Arnie said. "From now on, I'm going to consider that it means making the best move available to me, rather than worsening my position!"

"I like that shift in perspective," Dr. Pohl said. "Do you guys mind if I stay and watch? I love chess, and I haven't gotten to play for a while."

With that, Michael said, "I have a better idea. How about if you play against Arnie? I'm beat from working all day, and I wouldn't mind sitting back next to my friend Brandon here and watching."

"If you're sure that's okay? I would love a game."

"Please, have a seat," Arnie said. "Would you like to play white or black? Or, with my old set, I should say cream-colored or dark green?"

"I will take dark green, thanks. This is a very cool, ancient set. Hand-carved, I see." As Dr. Pohl picked up Merlynn and studied her closely, he noticed his fingers were coated with a dark soot-like substance. Upon placing Merlynn back on the board, Dr. Pohl grabbed a napkin and wiped the remaining soot off his fingers.

"Oh, sorry about that," Arnie said. "I thought I cleaned them off. Sorry, Doc. Hey, Michael, remember when we couldn't find that queen and a pawn? Strangest thing happened. I found them under my couch covered in soot or something. I was sure I'd looked all over, but all of a sudden, there they were."

"That's crazy," Michael said. "I had a strange experience a few weeks ago as well. I found a huge feather—it looked like an owl's feather coated in soot—on the mantel over my fireplace. I can't believe an owl would have flown down my chimney into my house, but I have no idea how the feather got there. Oh, and there were two small, round marks next to it, one a bit larger than the other." At this same time, all four noticed dark marks on the chess board where Merlynn and QP had been placed. "Just about those sizes," Michael said, pointing at the rings.

The ever-creative artist Brandon jumped in. "Hey, I know, a big owl took those two chess pieces, flew them down Michael's chimney, then returned them under Arnie's couch!" They all got a good laugh about this fanciful theory of Brandon's, while Merlynn and QP laughed hysterically to themselves, knowing exactly how accurate it was.

As the game started, Dr. Pohl circled back to Arnie's comment about his great-great-grandfather's possible madness. "You know, Arnie, as for your great-great-grandfather maybe being ill … while I love this game, it does have a dark side of drawing people in to the extent that they can become obsessed with the game to an unhealthy level. There are many stories about great players who wound up institutionalized or with other emotional challenges. I guess chess is like most things in life: all things in moderation. Well, let me modify that comment, as I can't even say substances in moderation are okay for those with the addictive gene."

"Would it bother you if I asked about your presentation while you play?" Michael asked.

"Not at all."

"Good, thanks. I learned a lot about the disease of addiction tonight, and I really appreciate you coming. I'm convinced my daughter is an alcoholic, as was my dad, and I understand she's sick. But I still get really mad when she tells me she won't drink again, then does anyway. I just can't stand her lying to me."

"First, I'm sorry about your daughter, and I'm sorry that you were raised by an alcoholic parent. And trust me, I hear this concern about addicts lying a lot in my medical practice. Maybe this will help. Now, your daughter, what's her name?"

"Katie."

"Okay, thanks. While lying is part of the disease of addiction, to others and to ourselves, I don't think Katie is lying to you when she says she will stop.

She means it at the time. I know this all too well, as I have been in recovery for many years now. Cocaine was my drug of choice. Every time I told friends and loved ones I was done and would never use again, I meant it at the time. Then, heck, sometimes within a matter of minutes, the reptile part of my brain kicked in and I said to myself, 'I will stop tomorrow, just not today.' But I wasn't intentionally lying at the time I said I was done using."

"Wow, that is interesting and helpful," Michael said.

"Thanks. So please don't get angry with anyone when they say they will stop and fail to do so. Now, it is okay to get angry. Just get angry at the disease of addiction that has taken hold of your loved one, not at them directly."

The game progressed, and Arnie realized he was up against a formidable opponent in Dr. Pohl. They exchanged pieces rather quickly and got to a fairly even endgame in no time. And— for the first time since becoming aware—QP played an important role, as Dr. Pohl got the upper hand by advancing her to the other end of the board and exchanging her for a queen. At this, Arnie knew the game was lost, resigned, and thanked Dr. Pohl for the invigorating experience. And QP, for the first time in her short life, felt really good about her accomplishments and the role she had played in a victory.

Brandon, Arnie, and Michael thanked Dr. Pohl for his talk. As Dr. Pohl headed for his car, Arnie asked Michael if anything was new at home.

"Yeah, pretty big change. Katie stormed out a couple weeks ago when I told her she could no longer drink in my house. Not sure where she is."

"Wow," Arnie responded. "Sorry to hear that. Are you okay?"

"Not really, sort of a hot mess. But I knew I had to do it."

Brandon chimed in, "I am sorry also. But, hey pal, you have my home number, right? And I'm pretty sure you have this old guy's number as well, to his rotary-dial landline, of course. You know, you could have called either of us at any time to talk, day or night."

"Yeah, good point. I probably should have called one of you. And I just might in the next couple of days. The house is really quiet."

"Please do," said Arnie, "on my cell phone!" He punched Brandon on the shoulder.

The three friends hugged and went their own ways. Michael felt really good knowing he could reach out to these guys if needed.

Meanwhile, to be expected, Goofus hated everything that had happened tonight, as he sensed his voice growing weaker.

Chapter 13

QP was feeling pretty good about having lasted until the end of the game and become a queen. But she was very subdued when they returned to The Cocoon.

Merlynn sensed there was something bothering QP and asked, "What's going on in that little bulb of yours?"

"Nothing, really. I'm fine."

"Fine? Fine, huh? Sorry, but it doesn't seem like it. 'I'm fine' is often a cop-out people use when they either are not in touch with their true feelings or do not feel their feelings are important enough to share with others. Do you remember when Megan was trying to get someone to share at a meeting a while back and—oh, wait, sorry, I think that was before you became aware.

"Anyway, there was a guy who never talked about what was going on with him during the family meetings. When it was time to share, he would pass or just say he was fine. Of course, it is acceptable to pass, especially when new to the meetings. But, after a couple months of him saying he was fine, Megan, insightful as always, decided to push him a bit—gently, of course. She reminded him of an acronym for the word *fine* often used in recovery circles. Do you know what that might be?"

"Nope. No idea."

"Okay, it stands for—and sorry for the crude language—when someone says they are 'fine' rather than sharing what is really going on, Megan said that can stand for Fucked-up, Insecure, Neurotic, and Exhausted."

"Fucking A! I love it."

"Hey, just because I used profanity in an example, don't think you have a green light to curse. You know I don't approve of that kind of language.

So, what's going on?"

"Okay, what bothers me is that all the stuff we heard earlier about the disease of addiction, what we saw with Michael's daughter leaving ... it's just all depressing. I'm tired of all this heaviness we listen to most of the time."

"I fully get it. Thank you for the candor," Merlynn said. "And that is true sharing of what you're actually feeling, rather than hiding it by saying 'fine.'"

"Another thing," QP said. "The people in these meetings have so many problems. Is it really good for them to be together so much? Sometimes it feels like they may build on each other's problems."

"Fair question. Actually, there are some in the recovery world who are not that supportive of recovering addicts hanging out together for the exact reason you just mentioned. Some feel it reinforces the idea that they're ill. While I get it, I don't agree. I have seen many benefit greatly from this community, and it sure beats being around people who are actively using drugs. Let's see if we can't find something lighter to focus on for today."

"Thank you. I am sick and tired of all this therapy stuff for now."

"Okay. Humor and not taking everything so seriously is important in this process as well. I have heard several funny stories and jokes over the centuries. Let's see what I can conjure up from this crusty old memory bank. Okay, who built the Round Table for King Arthur?"

Archimedes, still as small as a hummingbird tucked into a corner of The Cocoon, rolled his eyes, as he'd heard this way too many times. "Don't ask," he warned QP.

Merlynn didn't wait for permission to proceed, "Sir Cumference. And why wasn't King Arthur happy with the table?"

"Not sure I want to know," QP said.

"Because the carpenter cut some corners."

"No more, please!"

"You asked, and I am just getting warmed up. Why did I get really good grades in English?"

"No, not this one!" Archimedes said.

"Because I am really good at spelling."

QP and Archimedes both groaned and noted their disagreement with this one.

"My turn," Archimedes said. "Hey, QP, did you know I once beat a grandmaster in three moves?"

"I doubt that!"

"I did. It turns out he wasn't good at karate."

"Ugh, you are both terrible comedians," QP said. "Anything more substantive? I was talking about being depressed with all this darkness with addicts and stuff and about my own sadness, and these one-liners are not helping."

"Fair," responded Merlynn. "As I mentioned earlier, it is important to not take yourself so seriously, to find reasons to laugh and celebrate even in tough times. What do you think of when you hear the word *absurd*, QP?"

"You!"

"Ouch. Okay, seriously though."

"Something silly or stupid. Or very odd."

"Good, let's build on that as it relates to not taking ourselves so seriously," Merlynn said. "There was a philosopher, Albert Camus, who developed an entire theory of philosophy around the absurdity of life. His belief was that, while humans will always strive to figure out the meaning of existence, why they are here and so on, they never will be able to figure it out. He felt that trying to figure everything out was the cause of much suffering. But Camus also considered this quest to find answers for unanswerable questions inevitable. So his solution was to accept the absurdity of this situation. The story of Sisyphus is a good example of this."

"I remember you telling me about him," QP responded. "He was that guy who kept rolling a giant boulder up a steep hill, and every time he got it to the top, it just rolled back down again. I think he was destined to keep doing this forever. I can't think of anything worse."

"Good summary. But here is where Camus would disagree with your assessment of Sisyphus's situation. He argued that by accepting his fate, by not fighting against it, by fully embracing the absurdity, Sisyphus could actually be happy."

"Sounds sort of crazy to me. But it reminds me what we heard from Megan last month about the Serenity Prayer. About accepting what we can and cannot change."

"I see the similarities. And I find it sad that humans spend so much time and emphasis on differences between two ideas rather than focusing on their similarities. I mean, look at the many different religions. When you get right down to their main principles, they all have very much in common. But rather than celebrating this, humans get so bogged down in the subtle differences, they often wind up getting all judgmental and missing the whole point. Sort of the same with different recovery strategies.

"Sorry, I got sidetracked," Merlynn continued. "There is another branch of philosophy, referred to as Stoicism that some people have found very helpful in their recovery. It is sort of accepting things as they are rather than fighting them. I think that Brandon guy, the receptionist at BARC, has found support from that school of thought. He used to play chess with Arnie a lot before Michael started coming to BARC. Maybe we will hear him share about that at some point.

"Here is a much more recent story about the importance of lightening up from another favorite book of mine, *The Art of Possibility*. The main premise of this book is that everything is invented, so why not invent something good?

"The story is about the CEO of a company who continued to get fantastic results in his business year after year. A consultant visited him to try to figure out the secret to his success. While he was talking to this CEO, an employee came in very upset about something, raising his voice, almost yelling. Very calmly, the boss pointed to a sign on his desk that read 'Rule Number Six.' This exasperated employee calmed down right away, thanked his boss for the reminder, and left the office.

"To shorten this story, this happened a few more times while the consultant was interviewing the CEO. He always pointed to the 'Rule Number Six' sign with the same calming results.

Finally, the consultant said, 'This is amazing. All you do is remind your employees about this "Rule Number Six" and they calm down. May I ask what "Rule Number Six" is?'

'Of course,' responded the boss. '"Rule Number Six" is Don't Take Yourself So Goddamn Seriously.'

'Wow,' the consultant responded. 'What are the other rules?'

'There are none,' was the CEO's reply."[1]

"I have a proposed rule," said QP. "How about getting this owl to take a bath once in a while. He's stinking up our entire bag."

Fortunately, Archimedes knew better than to take cheap insults like this personally. The wise old (and smelly) owl just shrugged it off of his feathers and decided to share a funny memory of a meeting at BARC.

"Hey, Merlynn. Do you remember that woman at the BARC meetings a few years ago who shared a funny version of the twelve steps? It was sort of what not to do."

"Ah, yes, I don't remember her name, and we probably shouldn't share it anyway. Let me see if I can pull that out of my memory bank. Here it is. It was called 'Twelve Steps Before You Work the Twelve Steps.' I can see them, but I know they are projected only in my mind, so I will highlight a few for you both. They start with 'we admit we are powerless over nothing' and then 'we come to believe there is no power greater than ourselves.' Another funny—or sad—one, depending on your perspective, is that of being ready to make others straighten up and do right, then taking revenge and getting even with others rather than making amends.[2]

Archimedes shared his observation that the biggest difference between this humorous list and the actual twelve steps was that the satirical one placed all the blame on others, while the real steps were all about accepting responsibility for one's condition.

"Exactly," Merlynn said. "I just remembered that Grandmaster Rowson actually wrote about the value of humor in his book *The Seven Deadly Chess Sins*. He talked about the need for an element of surprise, which is what often makes us laugh. We laugh because we find the punch line unexpected. He links this to chess by encouraging the breaking of predictable patterns to keep your opponent off guard.[3] That is pretty close to what we have heard Arnie and Michael talking about. They often talk about the need to try new things—to experiment with new ideas in their own recovery."

"I just thought of a couple of recovery-related jokes," Archimedes said. "Okay, here goes. When you become a parent, you have to stop drinking if it's a problem. I mean, you can't come home at 2:30 a.m. and say to your kid, 'Here's a switch. Daddy's gonna throw up on you for a change.'"

Despite the groans from his two Cocoon mates, he continued undeterred.

"Okay, one more. An alcoholic is driving home from the bar at 3 a.m., totally annihilated. She's swerving between lanes and gets spotted by a patrol officer, who then pulls her over. The cop asks the inebriated woman where she's headed at such a late hour.

The drunk replies, 'I'm just going to a lecture, officer.'

In disbelief, the officer asks, 'Who would be giving a lecture this late?'

The alcoholic replies, 'My husband.'"

"That's enough, Archimedes," Merlynn said. "How are you feeling, QP?"

"A bit better. I do know I need to stop taking everything so seriously. I have been trying to control way too much that is out of my actual control. And I know I tend to be a jerk at times … well, most of the time. But I do appreciate our time together, and I've learned a great deal from both of you. So thanks."

Chapter 14

Arnie was just wrapping up a game of chess with his twenty-five-year-old grandson, Duncan, and had about two hours before he needed to head to BARC for the family meeting when his phone rang. He was pleased to hear Michael's voice on the other end rather than the all-too-frequent callers about his car warranty. He was equally pleased when Michael asked if he could meet him at BARC half an hour or so before the meeting, as he wanted to talk with him about something. After confirming it wasn't a crisis situation—in which case Arnie would have gone to meet him right away—they agreed to show up at BARC early.

They arrived at the same time and received their customary warm greeting from Brandon. Arnie asked if there was an open empty meeting room where they could talk for a bit.

"Sure, room B is empty and unlocked," Brandon said.

As they started to walk away, Brandon called out, "Hey, Michael, I know you're super busy in the summer months, but BARC is closed for the months of July and August. Did you know Dead & Company is playing a couple hours away on August twentieth? It'd be great if you could come with me. I'm picking up a friend of mine about halfway there who I think you'd enjoy meeting, and I have an extra ticket. I would love the windshield time with you."

"Oh, thanks. I'd love to spend time with you and hear that band. But I am super busy. I am not sure I can get away for an evening."

As Michael spoke, he glanced at Arnie and caught the roll of his eyes that said, *How about if you start putting yourself first for a change?* He reconsidered. "You know what, going to the concert is exactly what I need. Let's plan on it!" he said.

"Fantastic! I will text you all the info."

With that, Arnie and Michael entered room B.

"What's up?" Arnie asked.

"Well, interesting development with my son, Billy. Do you remember he's been missing for several months? And he has some mental challenges?"

"Of course. What's going on?" Arnie said. "First, though, thanks for calling me. That's what we're all about here."

"Well, sort of good and bad news," Michael said. "I got a call yesterday that he's in jail in a town about five hours north of here. Drug possession, panhandling, and resisting arrest. Sounds like he was sort of crazy and fought the cops a bit."

"Oh, sorry. Is he still in jail?"

"Yes. I took a call from him. I hesitated a bit at first, as I remembered something that stunned me a month ago," he said. "I think I mentioned I go to those NAMI meetings when I can?"

"National Alliance on Mental Illness? Yes," Arnie said.

Michael nodded. "There are a lot of parents there trying to cope with their kids with bipolar issues and stuff like that. This woman—oops—I almost said her name. Anyway, we were talking after the meeting about how her daughter had been missing. Her cell phone rang, and she looked at it but didn't answer it. She said it was the jail and she was glad her daughter was safe. She went right back to our conversation. She said she's been through it several times and wasn't going to stop our discussion to take the call. I couldn't do that."

"It's not about competition, you know. It sounds like she's been through a lot, and every situation is different. It seems like a good thing, to me, that your memory of that encounter gave you pause before you took your son's call."

"I guess. It was really hard knowing he was locked up, but he sounded better than I thought he would. He really wants me to come up and bail him out—when he can get out. I guess he gave someone at the jail permission to speak with me, because they told me later he was being held for a three-day evaluation. They were concerned because he had threatened to kill himself. I haven't slept much since, and I don't know what I should do."

"Understandable. You have a couple days to decide what to do, so that's a good thing. And remember, there is no *should* here. The question is, what do you want to do? The 'maybe good, maybe bad' story we talked about before comes to mind. This could be the beginning of something good for Billy."

"I hope so," Michael said. "And look here ... you know me well enough

"… I wrote down my feelings and have a list of pros and cons about going to get him. I tried to list all the options. And I actually tried to write about how I'd feel about it for a change, rather than just focusing on him."

"That sounds pretty darn healthy to me. And you know, I believe all things happen for a reason. Maybe it's just a coincidence, but I find it a sign of providence that we have a special guest speaker tonight on the exact stuff you and Billy have been going through. It's Dr. Pauline Boss, who developed a way to cope with a unique type of loss she refers to as 'ambiguous loss.'"

Michael surprised Arnie with this yet-unseen sense of humor as he said, "Hold on here, are you pulling my leg? Am I in a Doctor Seuss book? *Doctor Boss on Ambiguous Loss*? What's next month, *Oh, the Places You'll Go After Rehab*? Or no—how about, *Hop on Pop to Get Him Off the Pot*?"

"You are on a roll tonight, Michael, especially after having had no sleep. A little too much coffee? It's great you still have a sense of humor. Let's go grab some seats, as I am pretty sure it'll be packed. Hopefully we can talk more after the meeting."

As they walked down the hall, Arnie recalled that Michael's daughter, Katie, had stormed out of the house last month. "Anything new with Katie? Man, you've had some drama with your kids the past couple months."

"For sure. Well, I haven't seen her. She did at least let me know she's staying with a friend. She's still really pissed off, and she doesn't want to talk with me or see me. I've gotten healthy enough to know that's on her."

"Good job," Arnie said. They entered the crowded room just as Megan was introducing Dr. Boss.

"Good evening, and welcome to our Wednesday-evening family support group meeting," Megan said. "As I see some new faces, which is wonderful, this is normally a meeting where we talk about a topic and then have time for sharing. But we are honored tonight to have a special guest speaker who will share her thoughts on ambiguous loss with us. I am pleased to introduce Dr. Pauline Boss. Dr. Boss is a professor of family school science at the University of Minnesota and a psychotherapist in private practice. She has written two books on ambiguous loss, a concept she developed. She has graciously agreed to stay after her talk and sign copies of her book, *Ambiguous Loss: Learning to Live with Unresolved Grief*, for anyone who would like one. Please join me in welcoming Dr. Boss."

***

Dr. Boss spent the evening on an introduction to ambiguous loss.

She explained that ambiguous loss was just as it sounded—a loss that felt uncertain or unclear. She'd originally developed the concept to help family members and loved ones of armed-service members listed as missing in action deal with their grief. This concept of grief was subsequently expanded to address several other types of trauma, such as coping with losing a loved one to dementia, mental illness, or addiction.

She ended by reading a passage from her book:

People living with ambiguous loss are filled with conflicting thoughts and feelings. They dread the death of a family member who has been hopelessly ill—or mysteriously missing for a long time—but they also hope for closure and an end to the waiting. They may even feel anger at someone they love for keeping them in limbo, only to be consumed by guilt for having such thoughts.[1]

Dr. Boss explained several other aspects of coping with this unique type of loss, then shared coping strategies. Many were similar to the healing techniques Michael had learned about at the family support meetings and at the SMART Recovery meetings: finding group support, being realistic about how much control one has over the situation, and—as hard as it might be—taking care of oneself and continuing to do the things that bring pleasure despite the ongoing trauma. She concluded her remarks with one more passage from her book:

Becoming aware that someone we care about is neither here nor there is tragic. But, at the same time, ambiguous loss can, in spite of high stress, produce some good. In the confusion and lack of rigidity lie opportunities for creativity and new ways of being that have some purpose and a chance for growth.[2]

While she spoke to a large group, Michael felt as if she were talking directly to him. Her remarks struck home with everything he'd been feeling about his son. And he was thrilled to have the opportunity to thank her personally when he got to the front of the line to buy one of her books.

***

At the end of the meeting, Michael and Arnie made their way to the break room for their monthly game of chess. Michael was surprised to see the brand-new, very expensive, fully stocked Keurig machine on the counter. "Wow, look at this. Who paid for it?"

"Yeah, strangest thing. I asked Brandon about that the other day, and he said it just showed up. We must have a secret donor with deep pockets. Even stranger, Brandon said he locked up the night before it showed up, and it was here when he opened up the next morning. Maybe we have a ghost or a wizard or something?"

Still in The Cocoon, QP heard this and nudged the knowing Merlynn with her base.

Michael spoke. "You were right about Dr. Boss's talk being perfect for me tonight. It really hit home when she talked about feeling incompetent. I've felt like a terrible father because I can't seem to find an answer for Billy's situation. I've felt so out of control. Not even knowing where he was … there was nothing I could do to help him. It just didn't seem fair."

"There is nothing fair about it. And don't beat yourself up for feeling that way. That shows how much you love him. I went through a good deal with my wife's addiction, but she never went missing on me. So I have never been through that, and I can't imagine. I'm glad you found her talk helpful. Her book looks interesting."

"Yeah. The way she talked about needing to find meaning in other things in your life and the importance of connecting with others … I agree with that, for sure. All of this would be harder if I hadn't met you and other people here."

Michael continued. "And, hey, I was also thinking the other day that I've been pretty darn selfish. You know everything about me and my problems, and I hardly know anything about you. I never even bother to ask what's up with you."

"Well, look at you. Even though you are going through really hard stuff, you're asking about others. Dude—wait, am I too old to say 'dude'? Showing interest in others is a huge sign of growth."

"Thanks. I mean, I know you lost your wife several years ago and she had a drinking problem, but I don't even know about your family or what you did."

"Thanks for asking," Arnie said. "I retired, gosh, more than fifteen years ago now. I taught at the community college for about twenty years and elsewhere before that. Math was my subject. I'm sort of a geek that way. Maybe that's why I like this game of chess—I see math patterns in it."

"All I see is a bunch of squares and you taking my pieces. Do you have family?"

"Yes, I'm super blessed with two great kids and three grandchildren who are all doing well. Actually, my grandson, Duncan, comes over about once a month and plays chess with me. He's a real computer geek and a great mathematician. He knows more about math than I ever did, that's for sure. I hope you can meet him someday."

"That would be great. And that's cool that he spends time with you. Maybe none of my business … but I've been reading a bit about the impact of being an adult child of an alcoholic. You know my dad drank all the time, and he was a mess. I think it messed me up. Were your kids affected by your wife's drinking?"

"Good question. No, not while they were growing up, anyway. My wife's drinking problem didn't start until she was about fifty. It happened slowly. After the kids were gone, she stayed busy with some of her charity work but eventually lost her sense of purpose, I think. So, tragically, she turned to booze to escape. Both of our kids were really good about explaining her condition to their kids. We kept no secrets about her illness, which I think helped them understand."

"Wow, thanks for sharing," said Michael.

"Thanks for letting me share." They chuckled about using these sayings, common in the meetings they attended.

Chapter 15

Back in The Cocoon, QP was thinking about the conversation she'd heard between Michael and Arnie about Billy, Michael's son.

"Hey Merlynn, you awake over there?"

"Yes. What's up?"

"I think I worry way too much," QP said. "Hearing Michael talk about his son—how he worries about the right thing to do—made me realize I spend most of my time thinking about how to control others."

"Worrying too much about what others may or may not do is part of the disease of codependency," Merlynn said. "And let's work on that. I will start by sharing something I'm not sure I've told you yet. I hope you don't get mad at me for this, but when I brought you into awareness a while back, I screwed up part of the chant. I meant to instill in you 'independence' and wound up asking for 'codependence.'"

"Well, that figures," QP said. "A few months ago I might have been angry about this … but I'm really trying not to take everything so seriously, as we talked about a couple weeks ago. Rule Number Six, right?"

"Good memory! Thanks for leaving the vulgarity out of that rule. And for not being upset with me. I have felt bad about messing up the first two letters of that word. Thinking about definitions reminds me of something I heard a long time ago. Do you know the difference between guilt and shame?"

"No idea," QP said after thinking about it for a bit.

"Okay, sharing my feelings about how I messed up the chant when you were becoming aware is a good example of the difference between guilt and shame. While I feel bad about my mistake, I understand I merely made a mistake. Yes, I feel guilty I screwed up, and I have been working on making up for that in our lessons. However, that mistake doesn't make me a bad wizard. If I felt like I was a total screw-up because of that mistake, that would be taking on shame.

"Actually, an author I really respect, Dr. Claudia Black, said it much better than I just did in her recent and fantastic book, *Undaunted Hope: Stories of Healing from Trauma, Depression, and Addictions.* She was one of the pioneers in identifying family systems around the disease of addiction. I think she has written at least sixteen books and has dedicated her life to helping others heal from trauma."

"She sounds interesting and knowledgeable," QP said.

"She is for sure. Let me see if I can pull up the exact quote, as she said it better than I can. Here we go ... she wrote, "People often confuse guilt and shame. Yet, there is a fundamental difference between the two. Guilt is synonymous with remorse. It is what we feel when we realize we have made a mistake. Toxic shame is the feeling we have when we believe we are the mistake."[1]

"I see the difference," QP said. "And, while I'm not happy you made a mistake, I don't think you're a bad wizard because of it." She paused. "Scary and smelly, yeah. But you do have some redeemable qualities we can work on."

"Well, you are taking this 'keeping a sense of humor' stuff to heart, I see," Merlynn said. "I am not sure I appreciate the comments, but I will let them go for now. Until my next spell, at least. I think a good deal of you being overly controlling is tied into codependency and shame. According to Dr. Black, much of this comes from lessons people learn from dysfunctional family systems, and it can take a lot of hard work to overcome a negative self-image. If a person is told by their parents or someone else at a young and vulnerable age that they are a bad person, that tends to stick with them. Often, that is why people turn to drugs or other harmful ways of trying to escape—because they feel so bad about themselves."

"Merlynn, you mentioned trauma earlier, and I've heard Megan talk about that often in the family support meetings. I still think of trauma as a car accident ... or getting beat up ... or getting knocked off of a chess table, bouncing around on the floor, and winding up in a pool of old coffee, or something like that."

"You are making it very easy for me to stay in the memory bank I opened up about Dr. Black's recent book, which includes a good section about the type of trauma we are talking about here. And yes, you have a good memory of the first chess game after you became aware, when you wound up knocked to the floor. Maybe that is a sign of how vulnerable you were back then?" Then the queen, indulging her own sense of humor, said, "But hey, if it happens again, at least you will land in higher quality coffee and won't smell like Maxwell House instant."

"Ha. Yeah. Manifesting that Keurig coffee maker in the break room was genius."

Merlynn got back to teaching. "Here is how Dr. Black explained two types of traumas. She draws a distinction between what she refers to as 'Big T' trauma and 'little t' trauma. The 'Big T' traumas are like the ones you just mentioned and several others, including war, terrorism, any act of violence, incest, and neglect, to name a few. But Dr. Black stresses that the 'little t' traumas can be just as devastating to one's emotional and physical health. They include harsh or unfair criticism; being bullied, shamed, or demeaned; going through a difficult divorce; and many others. All require healing."[2]

"That's helpful," QP said. "Looking back again on the first chess game I remember, I think it still bothers me that Arnie said I was only worth one point compared to the other pieces. I think that messed me up."

"Acknowledging that is huge, QP. And you know I really do not like that ranking system or others like it. I think we can get so caught up in things like ranking systems, we often miss the bigger picture. You are worth way more than one point. Remember, you won that game for Michael a few months ago when you became a queen."

"That was fun, for sure. And it feels good talking about it with you. Just talking helps at times."

"I agree, with one suggestion. Let's remove the word *just* before the word *talking*. Talking is important; there is nothing *just* about it. It bothers me when I hear someone say, 'I am just this' or 'I am just that,' because in doing so, they are diminishing their role, whatever it may be. Our self-talk, the messages we tell ourselves about ourselves, is super important. We need to have more positive self-talk going on in our heads ... or crowns ... or bulbs, in our case."

This mention of self-talk reminded QP of something she'd read in a book Merlynn had mentioned to her. "Do you remember that book you told me about before, *Dashboard Bagels: Dishing Up Food for Thought*?"

"Of course, by that really handsome and humble author, Lance Wilson."

"Well, that analogy proves you need new spectacles and a cognitive test, but yes, that guy. I manifested a copy of his book just like you manifested the coffee machine, and there's a chapter about self-talk and worry."

"Ah, I love your budding confidence and desire to learn. Seems like the student is becoming the teacher. Please proceed."

"Okay, *Dashboard Bagels* has a chapter called "Green Card," in which the author tells of a time he got a certified letter in the mail and spent all night worrying that it was bad news."

"I remember that chapter. I learned that a human has to go to the post office to sign for a certified letter and that they put a notice in your mailbox at home—usually a small green postcard."

"Yes, right. So, when Mr. Wilson went to the post office the next morning, exhausted after having gotten very little sleep, he opened the letter and discovered a much unexpected check for twelve hundred dollars! As I remember, there was false advertising associated with a condo he'd recently purchased, and the check was compensation for that fraudulent statement. His moral of the story was to try to avoid worst-case-scenario thinking when you don't know the outcome of an upcoming event. Whenever he catches himself starting to worry, he chants 'green card' in his head to try to change the direction of his thoughts. He encouraged readers to come up with their own slogans or chants for that purpose, something from their own experiences. I think mine is going to be 'queen me' as a reminder that I can become anything if I set my mind to it."

"I am thrilled you are taking that approach. You are blossoming before my very eyes."

"Well, I'm not sure about that. I still worry a lot, and I wish I could stop. Any suggestions?"

"I am seldom at a loss for suggestions. My ideas are not that different from much of the stuff we have talked about already, like remembering what you truly can and cannot control and, as you just said, not taking yourself and everything so seriously. But here are a few more concrete action steps I have observed humans do over the years.

"Meditating or taking several deep breaths to relax your mind and body can help with worrying. I know that many people and even chess pieces I have made become aware don't feel able to sit still enough to formally meditate. If you find you are like that, that's okay. Maybe try taking five or six deep breaths and slow them down as much as possible if you are feeling anxious. I have found that to be helpful.

"Another idea that may help is to try to remove yourself from the situation. If you can remove yourself physically, try moving to a different part of The

Cocoon. Or, try to think of something more pleasant to remove yourself emotionally. Try pretending you are watching a play unfold and you are not involved. By doing this, you can become more like a passive observer, which helps you take whatever is going on less personally. When you do this, focus on why you may be reacting to whatever is going on around you, instead of stewing about why others are doing the thing that bothers you. And remember, if someone acts out or insults you, that is a sign of something going on with *them*, not a true or fair reflection of *you*."

"That is good advice," QP said. "We sure have heard Michael talk about worrying a lot about his kids lately. How he was lying awake at night worrying all the time. Well, now his son is in jail, and, like Arnie said, maybe that could be the start of something good for him. So was all that time Michael spent worrying a waste of time?"

"A quick answer is 'yes,' but I think that answer is too harsh. While his worrying may not have changed the outcome of the situation, I think we need to grant him—and others in his situation—generous grace. When you love someone as much as Michael loves Billy and Katie, it is difficult to not worry about them. To put a more positive spin on this, we can look at what Michael has done for himself despite the significant challenges with his family. He is here and learning so much, stepping out of his comfort zone. He has also grown his business, and he is not so preoccupied with things largely out of his control."

"Wow, good point," QP said. "I wasn't trying to be critical of him. I really like him. I was just curious."

"I know. I heard someone say once in a BARC meeting that while they were heartbroken about their loved one's addictions, they were not going to let that take them down. They understood that the job of addiction is to kill the addict—and to kill as many others as it can. They said they were not going to give their loved one's illness that much power over them, because then the addiction would be killing both of them. They would continue to live their life. But they also said they set aside a few minutes each day as 'worry time' to try to get it out of their system."

"I like the 'worry time' idea," QP said. "I will try that. I also think I need 'forgiveness time' for all the times I've been a jerk to you."

"Not sure we have that much time," Merlynn responded with a loving wink.

Chapter 16

Whether an act of providence or just a coincidence, Merlynn and QP had just been talking about forgiveness when Megan opened the monthly family support group meeting with this question: "Who do you need to forgive?"

Fortunately, only Michael could hear Goofus' answer as he jumped up and down and yelled, "This stupid guy whose shoulder I'm on needs forgiveness for bringing me here!" (Perhaps you noticed we hadn't heard from Goofus in a while. He was still there, but thankfully, his voice was growing quieter and quieter by the month.)

A few attendees, mostly those newer to BARC, offered answers:

"My wife, who won't stop drinking."

"My children, who are driving me nuts."

"The drug dealer who got my kid hooked."

"Myself," Michael said. "I need to forgive myself for feelings I still have that somehow I caused my kids' problems—and for thinking I can fix them. I sort of know better. I know I can't fix anyone else, but I still feel some guilt about their situations."

After thanking Michael for these insights, Megan circled back to the others who had offered different answers. "Thanks to the others who weighed in as well. I want to stress that there is no right or wrong answer to this question. I certainly understand and respect all the answers given. I do ask that, for our discussion tonight, we place more focus on Michael's answer—that the person we need to forgive first is ourselves."

A first-time attendee, highly emotional and not shy, chimed in. "I'm not the one smoking pot and skipping school and getting in trouble. I don't get it. What do I need to forgive myself for?"

"Fair point," Megan said. "I hear you loud and clear. Yes, we may need to forgive others as well. My point is that we first need to forgive ourselves. Especially if we feel in some way responsible for the addict's illness.

"If we feel like we need to forgive an addict, let's focus on forgiving them for being ill." She paused. "As I say that, it sounds odd to me—and I've been doing this for a long time. These are messy topics, so let me try to rephrase that. Would you feel the need to forgive someone if they had a tumor? Likely not. Now, that doesn't mean we don't have the right to be angry about choices addicts and others make. We do. But let's put the anger where it belongs: at the disease of addiction, not at the person."

Megan read the room and, sensing it was okay to proceed, asked what she trusted would be a more straightforward question. "Who do we harm the most by not forgiving others and ourselves?"

Several attendees simultaneously gave the answer she'd hoped for: "Ourselves."

"Yes," Megan continued. "We only hurt ourselves by not forgiving others. And only through forgiving ourselves can we begin to heal. Forgiving ourselves helps us not to play the victim role or become martyrs. Also, let's remember not to treat forgiveness as a deal or a barter-type situation. If we forgive expecting something in return from someone else, that usually leads to disappointment."

Arnie reached down to his bag, withdrew a dog-eared book he carried with him frequently, and asked if he could share something.

"Of course," Megan said.

"Thanks. This book, *Falling Upward: A Spirituality for the Two Halves of Life*, was given to me by the author several years ago when I was at a retreat of his in New Mexico. Not that I'm anywhere near the second half of my life, of course."

After the laughter subsided, Arnie continued, "I won't take the time to find the actual quote but, in here, Father Rohr writes something like, once we have forgiven ourselves, we then need to shift our energies to forgiving everybody else. He says if we don't do this, we will continue to judge others way too harshly.[1] That's the last thing I want to do, which is why I often come back to this quote."

"Thanks, Arnie," Megan said. "This reminds me of a story I heard at a conference I attended not long ago about how we only harm ourselves by harboring resentment. The title of the keynote address was 'Embracing the Hot

Mess,' and the speaker told a story from his book, *Dashboard Bagels*, about a broken plate."

While QP was in The Cocoon at Arnie's feet, she could still hear Megan and recognized the story from the same book she'd just read. QP wondered if this was more coincidence or more providence.

"The gist of the story is that, while cleaning up after a potluck party, the speaker accidentally broke someone else's plate. When he went to apologize, the person really went off on him, yelling about how the plate was an irreplaceable family heirloom. The speaker shared that he'd remained angry at this person's reaction for several years until he realized he was only hurting himself by hanging on to this ancient memory. Plus, he realized this person's reaction had nothing to do with him, nor even, likely, the actual event. It was more about whatever was going on in the other person's head. Then he also had to forgive himself for holding on to that resentment for so long in order to release its power over him."

An attendee chimed in. "Does anyone remember that terrible shooting of the ten young Amish girls several years ago?" Several people nodded. "I was amazed, and still am," he continued, "that right after the shooting, the Amish forgave the shooter. If I recall correctly, they actually went and comforted the shooter's family, as they knew their grief must have been huge also. I think I read that there were more Amish people at the shooter's funeral than non-Amish. I don't think I could do that if someone killed my child."

Megan thanked the person for sharing. "I agree. I doubt any of us can fathom that pain. I also think I would struggle with that level of forgiveness and grace. It does serve as a good example of what we are capable of, even under the weight of horrific grief.

"I know some of you in this room attend Nar-Anon meetings. A central part of the twelve-step recovery process they follow is taking an inventory and making amends to others when needed. Making amends to ourselves is an important part of that process as well."

"Can I share something that may be on point here about my son, Billy?" Michael asked.

"Of course," Megan said. "I was just wrapping up my comments and about to open up the meeting for sharing."

"Well," Michael said, "I may have talked with a couple of you about the fact that my son, Billy, had been missing for several months. I found out last month he was arrested in a city several hours from here. I was both glad to know he was okay and pissed off that he was in jail.

" I stopped being angry when they told me that they identified he was bipolar and needed medication and treatment. I guess I knew he was sick, but hearing it from professionals helped me stop being angry with him. Being here the past few months helped me understand that it's okay to be angry at his illness. But being angry at him won't really help, will it?"

"Wow, that's heavy stuff, Michael," Megan said. "And, yes, like I said earlier, we wouldn't be mad at someone who has a tumor, but it is okay to be angry about the illness. Are you comfortable sharing what's going on with him now and how you're feeling about it?"

"Sure. It's actually pretty good. Billy agreed to go to a hospital for treatment for a few days, and they recommended a group-home setting to help him stop self-medicating until he gets stabilized on medication. He agreed, which I was surprised to hear, but I'm really glad he did.

"I think insurance covers another thirty days, and then I'm not sure what happens. I talked with him once, with a counselor from the place where he's living. They don't want a lot of contact with family for now. He wants to come home once he gets out. I want him at home, but I'm sort of scared because I'm not sure what will happen or what's best for him."

"It's good that you have a few weeks to decide what to do. Any ideas what you need to do for yourself to help figure this out?"

"I've already shared some thoughts with and gotten guidance from a few others here. I am a list maker, and I've been writing pros and cons for my choices. A few months ago, I wouldn't have thought I even had a choice."

The not-shy newcomer who'd spoken earlier chimed in. "You don't have a choice. You have to let your child come home. Right?" He looked to Megan for affirmation.

Megan gently reminded him of one of the ground rules of the meeting, that of listening with an open mind and refraining from telling others what they needed to do. She also saw this as a learning opportunity for this new attendee and for others. "May I interject here, Michael?"

"Sure."

"Thanks. If I recall, your son is in his mid-twenties so he is far from a child. I have grown children as well, and I know that while it's never an easy decision, permitting them to return to your home is not always the best thing for them. And the more important question is if it's the best thing for you. Putting ourselves first is hard for many of us in this room, especially if we come from dysfunctional family situations where we were not taught the value of boundaries. Does anyone else have any thoughts or experience with this they'd like to share? Without telling Michael what he should or shouldn't do, of course."

"Not really a new idea for Michael," an attendee said, "but I do think we get resentful and feel violated if we set boundaries and then don't enforce them."

"Exactly," Megan said. "Then, often, we take this resentment out on others, which only makes a bad situation worse. I also suggest, if you set boundaries, to practice an anticipated discussion with someone you trust before you talk with your loved one about it. These are hard discussions, and you need to be ready for pushback."

"Sorry if I'm taking too much time tonight," Michael said, "but this is exactly what happened with my daughter not long ago. She opted to leave when I told her she could no longer drink in our home. It was and still is hard. And I probably shouldn't share this, but I'm sort of enjoying the peace and quiet. Which is one reason I have mixed feelings about Billy coming back home."

"You have had a lot on your plate, Michael," Megan said. "I love your candor and how you share so openly. And your feelings are very healthy, so don't beat yourself up over them."

"Thanks. I have become pretty good at not beating myself up. My energy at beating someone is going toward this guy here"—he pointed at Arnie—"on the chessboard."

"Thanks for the reminder that we're overtime this evening. I appreciate all of you for being here tonight, and, as we say every month, keep coming back. Oh, also, as is posted, we are closed all of next month and the month of August. We do this every year to give everyone a break and for deep cleaning. Please pick up a list of other meetings around town if you don't have one already, and make sure you have others' numbers if you need to talk. I hope to see you in September."

***

"Hey, Arnie," Michael said as he approached him. "Ready for our game?"

"I'm sorry, not tonight. I'm really tired. I just haven't been feeling like myself the past few weeks. I think I need to head home."

"Oh, man, I'm sorry. Go get some rest, and we'll catch up in August."

"I know you're busy," Arnie said, "but since your house is empty, if you don't have plans for the Fourth of July, my family is coming over for a cookout, and I'd love it if you would come spend the day with us. My kids and grandkids would enjoy meeting you. Maybe we could catch a game then?"

"Wow. That's really nice. I would love to come. I was sort of dreading being alone on a holiday like that when most people are with their families."

"Deal. Come over any time after noon, and come hungry."

"Thanks. I hope you feel better."

Chapter 17

"I couldn't hear too well, being in The Cocoon the entire time at that meeting yesterday," QP said. "But it was interesting that the topic was forgiveness. We had just been talking about that."

"I agree," Merlynn said, as she moved out from behind Archimedes, who had decided to hang out with these two.

"I still am a bit mad at you for messing up the chant when you made me aware," QP said. "Now I have so many codependency tendencies, and I still need to work on forgiving you for that. It's hard for me to let go of resentment."

"Understood. You know I regret that mistake. What else do you think we can do to help?"

"Not sure, but I would love to get out of here for a bit. I'm getting tired of being in this bag. Can we go anywhere?"

"Are you up for a test flight, Archimedes?" Merlynn said. "If so, I know just the person we could visit to learn more about forgiveness."

"Sure," the owl said. "I have a feeling I know where we're headed. Let's keep the little one in suspense, but to confirm I'm on the right track, would Robben Island be our destination?"

"Exactly! Let's head out whenever you are ready."

Archimedes grabbed her two passengers in her talons, and took off across the ocean—and back in time a few decades. They arrived at their destination, and while squeezing through the slats of the upper window of a cell, Archimedes accidentally hit QP's head on one of the rusty bars.

"Ouch, what the hell?" QP said as she was rudely awakened from their flight. She saw that they were on a two-foot-thick stone ledge about ten feet up from the cell floor.

With this outburst, the prisoner who sat alone below, leaning over a chess board, looked up. "Well, hello, Archimedes. And, I trust that's my friend Merlynn beside you? I have not seen you as a chess queen before, but I like it! And who's your little pawn friend all covered in rust from the bars of my old cell?"

"Hello, Mr. Mandela," Merlynn said. "Yes, it is me. It is great to see you."

"Please, call me Nelson."

"Okay. This is QP. She has been with me a very long time, but she only became aware about six months ago. She is really smart and curious."

With that, much to QP's surprise, a rook on the chess board looked up and said, "Hi, Queen Merlynn. It's been way too long."

QP could no longer contain herself. "Do I have a concussion, or can this guy below us really see us? And is that rook talking to us? I must be dreaming or something, because no other human or other chess piece has been able to see us, let alone talk with us."

"Nice to meet you," Mr. Mandela replied. "No—I am sorry about your head—but you aren't imagining any of this. Merlynn, do you want to explain?"

"Sure. You are right, QP. This is one of the very few people I permitted to see us and to interact with Rookie down there. Hi, Rookie. I brought Rookie into awareness, gosh, twenty years ago, right after Nelson was arrested."

"I don't get it," QP said. "Why?"

"It's a long story. And, unfortunately, it has been a much longer one for Nelson. Where to start? We've flown to South Africa. Nelson has been fighting apartheid here for most of his life. He was arrested and sentenced to life for fighting for justice and, to use an ancient King Arthur idea, for right over might.

"I knew he was an extraordinary person, and I couldn't stand the idea of him being in here alone. That was when I brought my friend Rookie into awareness. I also knew we could trust Nelson to keep a secret, so I permitted him the ability to see us and communicate with us and Rookie."

"And I thank you for that!" Mr. Mandela said. "Rookie has been a godsend, as has all I have learned from him and about chess while I have been here. You did look like a more traditional wizard last time I saw you, but I understand that you take several different forms."

"That Rookie has helped you warms my wizard heart! Though I am strictly prohibited from telling the future, unfortunately, even though I have already lived through it, I will say this. Even though you were sentenced to life, I know you have spent far more time in here than you will going forth. You also have a bright future ahead of you."

"Well, thank you for that wonderful news. I have never given up hope."

"I bet you hate the people who did this to you," QP said.

Before Mr. Mandela could reply, Merlynn said, "Before you answer that question, Nelson, I brought QP here because we are learning about the power of forgiveness, and I know that is one of your many superpowers. So I hope you can share your thoughts on that subject."

"Of course," he said. "And, no, I do not hate anyone, as that is a waste of energy. I need all my energy for positive thoughts; otherwise I am only hurting myself. Hating only clouds the mind. I feel the same about resentment. I have often said that resentment is like drinking poison and then hoping it will kill your enemies.

"And not forgiving is equally hurtful to yourself. As hard as it has been in here, I have fully forgiven my captors. If I do not do that, I am giving them much more power over me than they already have, and I am not willing to do that."

"Wow," QP said. "And here I am having a hard time forgiving Merlynn for messing up the chant when she made me aware. She made me 'codependent' rather than 'independent.'"

"Dang. You got off lucky," Archimedes said. "Hey, Rookie, do you remember the time Merlynn brought that bishop into awareness and she confused the word 'intelligence' with 'belligerence'? What a mess that was!"

As Rookie chuckled at that memory, Merlynn chimed in. "I am tempted to erase your memory bank, Archimedes!" Then to QP, she said, "Nelson is saying much the same thing we heard at our last meeting from Megan and others about the need to forgive others. And, more importantly, to forgive ourselves."

"Don't get me wrong," Mr. Mandela said. "Forgiving others hasn't been easy. I admit I harbored some resentment for too long, and I had to forgive myself for that feeling to be truly free from negative thoughts. Initially, I was afraid of my fate. Of being locked up in a place like this, likely for the rest of my life. It took a long time to understand that my fear of the unknown was wasted energy as well."

Archimedes chimed in. "Hey, Merlynn, remember when we were in the White House and the president said something about being afraid? Something like, 'the only thing we have to fear is fear itself'?"

"Yes. That was President Franklin Roosevelt during his first inaugural address. President Roosevelt's full sentence was, 'So, first of all, let me assert my firm belief that the only thing we have to fear is fear itself—nameless, unreasoning, unjustified terror which paralyzes needed efforts to convert retreat into advance.'"[1]

"Thanks for sharing the entire quote, Merlynn," Mr. Mandela said. "I have often wondered why the rest of that quote was left off. To me, the most important part is the last clause—the importance of converting retreat into advance. I think action statements, or what we are going to do to make a situation better, are important.

"Being imprisoned has taught me that education is the most powerful weapon which you can use to change the world. I believe firmly that everyone can rise above their circumstances and achieve success if they are dedicated to and passionate about what they do. That is why I have focused my energy on action, on what I can do, rather than letting these bars limit me."

"Man, Mr. Mandela," QP said. "I can't believe you can be so positive in here. I get antsy just being in The Cocoon. I can't imagine what you have been through."

"Thank you. I wouldn't wish this on anyone. But I have learned that attitude is a choice. We always have a choice over how we think and how we react to situations. I try to stay focused on the positive. Are you familiar with Victor Frankl?"

Seeing the pawn shake her bulb in the negative, he said, "I suggest you read his book, *Man's Search for Meaning*. If I start feeling sorry for my situation, I reread that book, and it makes me realize how fortunate I am. Victor Frankl is a Holocaust survivor who spent three years in various concentration camps. He went on to become a noted neurologist and psychologist.

"The main message of *Man's Search for Meaning* is, as I just said, that we have a choice as to how we respond. He stresses his observations that those who survived those horrid conditions, those who never gave up hope, those who helped others even though they were starving were the ones most likely to survive. So I refuse to give up hope.

"Also, having Rookie here and knowing Merlynn is out there and can come by anytime has been a huge help as well."

"Thanks," Rookie said. "I enjoy being with you, as I certainly get a lot of use. We play almost every day. Not only does it help our attitudes, but I have also seen it help others."

"What have you been up to, Merlynn?" Mr. Mandela asked. "It has been several years since we saw each other. Where and in what time period are you three spending your time these days?"

"We are in the year 2024," Merlynn said. "We have been with a very interesting guy named Arnold Zugzwang for the past ten years or so."

"As a queen in a chess set, you sure picked a guy with the right last name," Mr. Mandela said to a round of chuckles.

"We did for sure. Arnie, as his friends call him, is a great guy. Oh, hey, I just remembered an interesting coincidence. Before we came to live with Arnie, we were with a guy, a grandmaster named Jonathan Rowson, who was asked how he thought you would be as a chess player. He said:

'When I think of what Mandela's story has to offer the chess player, I would say patience, because he was in jail for a long time; courage, because he had to believe in himself and his ideas when the position was hostile to both; and imagination, because he had to see several moves ahead to a position with new rules and pieces with new powers, and still believe he could keep control.'"[2]

"That seems accurate," Mr. Mandela said. "I am surprised people are still talking about me."

"No surprise," Merlynn responded. "As I shared, you have a bright and promising future ahead of you. Okay, back to Arnie. He is also using the game of chess and his years of experience to help many people. We hang out a lot at a recovery center for people dealing with addictions and mental illnesses and for family members working on overcoming the negative impact of these situations. He teaches many newcomers how to deal with challenging situations through chess parables."

"Sounds fascinating and a noble cause. You always have been a dedicated servant. And QP, what have you learned from this old wizard and her wise owl?"

"A great deal. One, to try to not let my bulb hit anything, that's for sure. But seriously, we attend many meetings at the recovery center, and I learn about how people deal with trauma and how to develop skills to overcome bad circumstances. I am still pretty insecure, though, and I am trying to work on my own confidence a bit."

"Thank you for your candor," Mr. Mandela said. "Building courage often takes time, practice, and a belief in yourself. Please keep that in mind, QP.

Also, remember when playing chess that a player is braver after the game.[3] I often catch myself thinking after the fact that I should have done this or that. And these post-mortem ideas are often bolder than what I did at the time. So, why not be bolder, more courageous at the time? Not reckless, of course, but a bit braver."

Suddenly, the lights began to flicker on and off, a warning that it was time for lockdown and quiet time. "I sure will be glad when I have control over when I go to bed and get up," Mr. Mandela said. "I have loved this visit, but unfortunately, we need to cut it way too short. As always, it was wonderful seeing you again, Merlynn and Archimedes, and very nice meeting you, QP. You are in very good company with these two, and I can sense your confidence building. Thank you for sharing with me."

"It has been wonderful seeing you both," Merlynn said. "Take good care of him, Rookie. We will come again."

With that, Archimedes grabbed Merlynn and QP in her talons, QP tucked in her bulb tightly, and they departed through the bars of the cell to make their way back to Marietown.

Chapter 18

Michael woke up excited about having the entire day off for the Fourth of July. He was also looking forward to spending the day at Arnie's home. Around ten in the morning, he received an unexpected phone call that brightened his day even more: a call from his son, Billy.

They talked for a good forty-five minutes. Billy sounded better than he had in years. He said he was enjoying his new living conditions, attending meetings, and working part-time. He also shared that he had a good therapist and was finding his new medications helpful.

"Dad, I got some good news yesterday. Remember I said insurance would only cover thirty days where I'm living? I just got approved for another thirty days, so I'm okay to stay here until around the end of August. I sure hope I can come home after that."

Michael was thankful that he and Arnie had prepared for this discussion. Despite having rehearsed this, it almost broke Michael's heart to not just say, "Of course you can come home."

"That's great news about the insurance, and I'm thrilled you are doing so well. I know you want to come home, and I hope you know I want that as well. I am pretty sure we can make that happen, but is there a way we can set up a couple of calls with your therapist or a social worker there before finalizing that? I just want to make sure you coming home is best for you and for me. I have really been working on myself the past several months, and I think it would be good to process this with a professional."

"I get it, Dad. I might not have a month ago or so. I am getting a better understanding for my feelings as well. So don't worry about saying that. I am okay with that approach. Let me see what I can set up here. Hopefully we can make that work."

"I know I am a crybaby," Michael said. "And, dang it, you made me bawl here. Tears of joy, I should note."

"Ha. Yeah, Dad, your sensitive side always comes through, for which I am thankful. Hey, I need to get off the phone. One of the counselors is taking a bunch of us to a park today for a cookout. I hope you have something planned."

"I do. I am headed to a new friend's house for the day. I hope you can meet him sometime soon. Thanks so much for the call. Go have fun!"

"Cool. Love you, Dad."

Michael wiped the tears away, continued to clean up the house, and started to focus on getting ready to head to Arnie's.

***

Arnie's door was opened by a middle-aged woman who welcomed Michael warmly. "You must be Michael. Dad has talked about you a lot, and he's excited about you being here. I'm Betsy, Arnie's daughter. Come on in."

"Thanks. It's nice to meet you. I love spending time with your dad."

"So do we! He and my son, Duncan, are just starting a game of chess in the den. Let me show you the way. Can I get you anything to drink or eat? There are snacks in there."

"I'm good for now. Thanks."

"Hey, Michael," Arnie said as they entered the den. "I'm so glad you're here. This is my grandson, Duncan. The true mathematician in the family I have told you about."

"Nice to meet you," Duncan said as he rose from his chair across from the chess set. "We were just going to start a game. Would you like to play instead of me?"

"No. Go ahead. I would love to watch, though, if that's okay."

"I guess that is all right," Arnie said. "Although I'm not sure I want you to see me get embarrassed by this young guy."

"That seldom happens," Duncan said as he opened by moving his queen's pawn up two spaces. Arnie responded with the same move, taking QP by her bulb and moving her right up against Duncan's queen's pawn. QP was happy to be back home and engaged in a game on familiar territory.

As the game progressed, Arnie said, "Before you came in, Duncan was telling me about something called the prisoner's dilemma, a game-theory principle, and how it can be applied to recovery and life choices in general. Are you familiar with the prisoner's dilemma?"

"Never heard of it. Do you mind giving me the dumbed-down version, Duncan?"

"I doubt he can dumb it down enough for you," Goofus said into Michael's ear. "And I can explain it faster. I am the prisoner, and my dilemma is having to be here with you!"

To which Gallant responded, "Shut up, Goofus. Sorry you can't handle a healthy situation in which you might have to learn something new. By the way, you seem to be getting shorter by the day. I can't wait until you disappear for good."

Michael quieted these inner voices in time to hear Duncan say, "I hardly think dumbing down will be necessary. But, yeah, sure. It is sort of the classic example of game theory. It starts with two people being arrested and the cops trying to get each one to flip on the other one. If one snitches on the other one, the first goes free and their partner in crime gets three years in prison. If they both stay silent, there is not enough evidence to convict them of the more serious charges, so they each get just one year in jail. But if both tell on each other, or cooperate with the cops, they each get two years in jail: a shorter sentence for cooperating. Oh, and they are in separate cells, so they can't talk to each other at all."

"Okay. Let me see if I get it," Michael said. "I have no idea what my friend will do. So, if I rat him out and he stays loyal to me, I go free but he gets three years. And it's just the opposite if I stay quiet but my partner flips on me. If we both stay silent, we each get one year. And if we both cooperate with the cops, we each get two years. Right?"

"You got it," Duncan said.

"Wow. That's a tough one. I guess the best thing for both of us is to stay quiet, as we'd each only get one year. But I would hate to stay loyal to him, then find out he flipped on me, because then he walks and I'm in jail for three years. What's the right answer?"

"There's no right or wrong answer," Arnie said. "That is where the dilemma lies. A general challenge of game-theory concepts is that decisions that may be best for an individual are often terrible for a group. For me, it makes me think about my self-interest versus what might be best for a group or for society. These things often seem to be in conflict with each other."

"So," Michael said, "I understand the challenge with two people in custody like this. But you said you were talking about how it might apply to other situations. Not sure I get that. That's a pretty unique situation, and one I don't plan on being in, for sure!"

"Neither do I," Duncan said. "The link to other situations may be a bit abstract. It requires shifting our thinking about the prisoner's dilemma from an external one, dealing with another person, to an internal one, dealing with our own thought processes. Or a good way to say it might be thinking about our present selves versus thinking about our future selves.

"Let's take overeating as an example," Duncan continued. "See this bowl of chips here? I would love to eat the entire bowl right now. That is what my present self wants. On the other hand, my future self doesn't want to get fat and have health problems down the road. So what I want right now isn't really in my best interest in the future."

"Okay, thanks. I sort of get it, I guess," Michael said. "It reminds me of when your grandfather shares chess quotes with me that reference the opponent. The opponent in chess is an external force, the person across the table. But when we talk about these chess ideas as they relate to life in general, we often talk about our internal opponents, our self-talk, rather than the opponents being other people. Gosh, listen to me, I am really getting out there. Does that make any sense?"

"Absolutely," Duncan said. "But I'm surprised to hear that Granddad uses chess quotes. News to me …"

"Watch it, Grandson. Enough of your sarcasm." Turning his attention toward Michael, Arnie said, "A few weeks ago, Duncan told me how a friend of his was finding game theory beneficial in his own addiction recovery. The link, as I understand it, is that game theory calls for one to look at future consequences of situations. When applied to recovery, if someone focuses on their future self, or what they want their life to look like down the road, this can help quell the urge to use today. Having hope for a brighter future is a key to staying clean. And, in our case, to overcoming our codependent tendencies as well."

"That makes sense," Michael said. "Actually, I did want to process something with you that happened this morning, Arnie. And these game theory ideas might help with this."

"Do you want me to step out?" Duncan asked.

"No. I would like your thoughts as well, as you are much closer to my son's age. And hey, I have no secrets or shame about what is going on in my life. I used to, but not anymore."

"What's up with Billy, Michael?" Arnie asked.

"He called this morning from his sober-living house. We had a great talk and he's doing fantastically, from the sounds of it. He got approval to stay another thirty days, which is great. He said he wants to come home after that. That is what I wanted your thoughts on."

"My first question is, how do *you* feel about that?" Arnie said.

Michael shared the discussion he'd had with Billy that morning and said that he felt pretty good about him coming home, but he just wanted to make sure it was the right thing for him and for his son. He asked Duncan if he had any thoughts and if game theory could be applied here.

Duncan said he didn't know all the intricacies of the situation to have an opinion one way or the other on what Michael should do. He asked if there might be a middle-ground solution. Maybe having Billy come back to town and start with him in a short inpatient program someplace close by so they could reestablish a relationship. Then, if that went well, possibly Billy could come back home and still attend some intensive outpatient program during the day.

"That's a good idea," Michael said. "I will look into various options and see if Billy will consider that."

"Nice," Duncan said. "There is a related game-theory concept called the 'Battle of the Sexes.' In this game, two people want to do different things, and a study examines different outcomes of the various choices. You might want to take a look at that."

"Okay, thanks."

"It's great you asked for our input on this, Michael," Arnie said. "As we have discussed, a key for our recovery from codependency is soliciting others' ideas and not just jumping into what feels right without looking at all options. And, as you said earlier, this is a pretty good decision to have to make, given where you both were a few months ago."

"You got that right," Michael said as Duncan pushed QP to the eighth rank of the board, exchanged her for a queen, and announced checkmate on his grandfather.

"Isn't it time for you to go home?" Arnie joked with Duncan. "I can't remember the last time I beat you. Let's go join the rest of the family. I need to get the barbeque going, anyway."

Michael spent the rest of the day getting to know Arnie's children and grandchildren and a few other friends who spent the day with them. He left feeling very conflicted. On one hand, he was full of gratitude for the wonderful day he'd spent with Arnie and others. On the other hand, he was sad knowing he was returning to an empty home, as he longed for this type of healthy family interaction in his own life.

Chapter 19

QP awoke excited, as this was the day they would start their long holiday journey. She was still stunned by what she'd learned last month from Nelson Mandela about the power of forgiveness and surprised at how much she was enjoying learning new things. She hoped to meet interesting people on this trip.

"Are you ready for some long-distance flying?" Merlynn asked Archimedes.

"Ready to fly!" the owl said. "I am glad I have had some rest with you after our trip to South Africa last month. Let's head out. Where to this time, Merlynn?"

"QP has been doubting our lineage, so we will visit a few people from our past. And as this will be my last journey with you, let's make it as educational as possible. Please try to drop in on our friends when we can learn something from them. QP has learned much, and I am loving her growth. But there is much I want to leave her with."

"What do you mean, this is your last trip with us?" QP asked.

Before Merlynn could respond, Archimedes helped out his long-time friend. "As the queen may have told you, she is aging backward and becoming very young. Soon she will slide back into the mysterious place from which she came, the wizard womb. But don't worry: I am timeless and will always be here for you."

"Well, Merlynn, just come up with some chant or spell to change that!" QP said. "I don't want you to disappear!"

"This was all cast in stone eons ago, well before King Arthur's sword was placed in the boulder. I can't change this. And while I will miss you, I wouldn't change this course of action even if I could. I am tired. I am looking forward to whatever type of rest lies ahead for me. Please remember what we heard recently about the futility of worrying about the unknown. Also, QP, I know your future. You will be fine. Not 'fine' in the forced, superficial sense that isn't helpful for recovery, but you will be better than fine. You will flourish past your wildest imagination."

"Okay. I don't like this one bit, but neither of you have let me down yet. I will try to not worry. Remember what that Wilson guy said about the certified-mail story and having a slogan or saying to try to avoid slipping into worst-case-scenario thinking? You know, when he repeated 'green card' to himself to help stop assuming the worst? I told you my saying was going to be 'queen me.'" With that, QP slipped into a quiet "queen me" chant as she worked on slowing her breathing.

"I wish I had been around for that talk," Archimedes said. "That guy sounds really smart." He flexed his wings. "Where to first?"

"Let's take our journey in chronological order so I don't get too confused," Merlynn said. "My earliest memory in this chess set goes back to when I was with King Louis IX in France around 1226. Let's start there."

"Let's not," Archimedes said.

"Why not?"

"Two reasons. First, you know how long it takes me to go back just one hundred years. I am not sure I can make it that far back. And don't you remember that King Louis IX banned chess as boring and useless?"

"Good point on both fronts," Merlynn said. "Okay, since not much happened after chess was banned, and we lay dormant for a few hundred years, let's skip that era. How about if we go visit that avid chess player, Charles I, king of England. Can you fly that far?"

"Sure, but ... you do recall the gruesome ending, right?"

"Hard to forget that, yes. While the king met a bloody mess of an ending, there's a valuable story there, so let's head out." With that, Archimedes grabbed her two friends gently in her talons and started the long journey across the ocean and back some four hundred years.

Upon arriving, the three time travelers found themselves observing King Charles I playing a game of chess with a friend. Suddenly, in barged one of his military advisors, who announced, "Your Majesty, I regret to inform you the Scots have changed sides and are now supporting Parliament. This requires your immediate attention."

Despite this dire news, the king ignored the warning and continued his game.

***

Over the next few weeks, Merlynn, QP, and Archimedes hung around and watched as King Charles I was tried and found guilty for treason and sentenced to death. Of course, while it was unlikely his refusal to stop his chess game was a key reason for his death sentence, historians speculated that it may have been one factor.

***

Later that night, Merlynn asked, "What do you think the moral of this story is, QP?"

QP thought for a moment. "I think the lesson is to not get so wrapped up in what you're involved in that you ignore the big picture. The king should have stopped playing his game upon hearing that bad news."

"Very good. Chess players often get into trouble that way. Not the kind of trouble that would result in having their heads cut off, thank goodness, but players do lose games when they get too focused on their attack and don't pay attention to their opponent's plan. I have witnessed this often in games throughout the centuries. A player thinks they have a solid attack, so they start to ignore the opponent's moves. It usually winds up backfiring on them."

"We have heard that discussed at the BARC meetings," QP said. "Megan often reminds attendees to look at all options before acting. And I think Michael has started to do that pretty consistently."

"Great observation," Merlynn replied.

"So," QP asked, "where did we go next? I think it was about another one hundred years before we wound up with Ben Franklin, right? What happened in between?"

"Not much to share during that time. Our chess set was passed around by several people for a while before we wound up with a sailor making his way across the Atlantic. I hated that journey, as I was seasick most of the time. We eventually landed in an antique shop in Philadelphia. That's when Ben found us: around 1730, I think? How about if we go visit Ben for real this time, Archimedes? Not Abe Lincoln!"

"Deal," the owl replied. "Since we are already across the Atlantic, I will take us to Mr. Franklin while he was serving as ambassador to France." Archimedes gathered his passengers and took off across the English Channel from England to Paris, advancing in time about a hundred years.

They arrived close to 10 p.m., and Archimedes gracefully navigated through an open window of the home of Madame Brillon de Jouy, a close friend of Mr. Franklin's and someone who, rumor had it, Ben wished were more than just a friend. To everyone's surprise and embarrassment, they looked down from their window ledge and saw the good Madame soaking in a bathtub while Mr. Franklin and another person sat beside the tub, engrossed in a game of chess. To the modern reader, this scene may seem more risqué than it was; back then, wooden planks were placed over the top of the tub for privacy.

Even with the wooden planks in place, QP started giggling. Merlynn was glad no one could hear or see them. This was not exactly where the wizard had wanted Archimedes to take them.

"Archimedes, really? Couldn't you have taken us to a different time and place with Mr. Franklin? One not quite so intrusive?"

"Sorry. I just set off for Ben like you said. Please be more specific next time."

Fortunately for all involved, the game ended within thirty minutes, and the three visitors secretly followed Mr. Franklin to his home, where they all slept soundly.

The following evening, his three house guests accompanied him to Café de la Régence, a legendary coffee house and gathering place for chess players in Paris. There, they had the pleasure of listening to Mr. Franklin as he discussed politics and life over a few games of chess with friends.

Ben was in quite the talkative mood that evening, something not uncommon for him when he played chess with friends over a few drinks. At one point, his opponent asked why he enjoyed chess so much.

"The game of chess," Ben responded, "is not merely played for fun and to kill time. Rather, chess teaches us many valuable skills like patience, learning to look ahead, and losing gracefully. Life itself is like a game of chess. We need all of these habits to succeed."

Mr. Franklin continued by sharing three aspects of chess he found useful in life: foresight, circumspection, and caution. Foresight, he said, required looking ahead and anticipating future moves, while circumspection involved looking around the board and considering all current probabilities. Finally, caution reminded players to avoid hasty moves, lest they wind up in bad positions. Ben reminded his playing partner that chess taught one even in a bad spot to maintain hope and look for opportunities for positive change. Most situations were not as dire as they seemed.

Upon hearing this, QP told her traveling companions that she had often heard the same three qualities discussed at BARC. This insight deepened her understanding of how chess principles applied to daily living.

***

After the trio had spent a few days in France, sometimes spending time in Mr. Franklin's company and sometimes sightseeing, QP asked Merlynn where the chess set had wound up next. Merlynn explained that much later in Mr. Franklin's life, he gave the set to Thomas Jefferson before Mr. Jefferson became the third president of the United States. After that, they spent more than two hundred years in the White House.

"Can we go hang out with Jefferson and all the presidents who played chess?" QP asked.

"Unfortunately, no. Arnie has been looking for us, and we need to head back home soon. When he found we'd gone missing again, he pulled out a small plastic chess set. I really should create some lookalike pieces to stand in for us when we travel like this. Let's get some rest this evening before heading back to Arnie's."

"Sounds good," QP said. "But, if I recall correctly, you talked before about how we were with Grandmaster Rowson for a while. When did we leave the White House, and how did we wind up with Mr. Rowson?"

"Good question. That happened in 2002 when Grandmaster Rowson tied for first place in the World Open in Philadelphia. At that time, George W. Bush was in the White House, and while he was a nice guy and well meaning, he was not much of a chess player. He was cleaning up the White House residence one day, sort of trying to stay busy, and he wanted to make room for his baseball collection. So he donated us as a prize for that tournament. He sure had to fill out a bunch of government forms to get that done. Well, someone else filled them out for him, of course."

"So, that's how we got to Mr. Rowson! And then he gave us to Arnie in that exhibition match, right?

"Yes," said Merlynn.

"Where will we wind up next?"

"I do know that, but I cannot share it with you. Trust me, you will enjoy the person you will be with next. One thing I can promise: you will never be bored, especially if you stay curious and a lifelong learner."

Chapter 20

Mid-August came quickly for Michael. He was swamped with his business, reading more about recovery from codependency, and practicing chess online. He felt guilty about leaving his crews early on a Saturday to get cleaned up to go to the concert with Brandon, but he knew this would be a well-deserved break. He was amazed when he realized this would be the second fun thing he'd done for himself in as many months, after attending the cookout at Arnie's last month. He couldn't remember the last time he'd done something other than work, worry, and pace the house trying to sleep.

It felt good to put himself first for a change, something foreign to him. He recalled Megan asking at one of his earlier meetings: "Who is the most important person in the room?" He now chuckled at his initial reaction as he'd looked around the room trying to figure out who she meant.

Michael drove across town to Brandon's and arrived right on time at four o'clock for the two-hour drive to the concert. He arrived just as Brandon was getting to his own car.

"Hey pal, jump in," Brandon said. "So glad you agreed to go tonight. Dead & Company is getting rave reviews for this concert tour and we have great seats."

"Cool. I need this. Been working way too hard. And I'm looking forward to chatting with you a bit before we pick up your friend—remind me of his name?"

"His name is Sam. He lives about halfway there, so we have an hour to catch up."

"Nice. You know, like I said to Arnie a few weeks ago, I've been so wrapped up in my own issues, I hardly know anything about him—or you. You guys have heard all my crazy family stuff the past several months. I've been pretty selfish to not ask how you're doing. Heck, other than knowing you're a great artist and volunteer at BARC, I don't know much else about you. Sorry."

"No need to apologize. You've had a lot on your plate. And I'm pretty boring anyway."

"I doubt that. Seriously, how did you get involved in BARC? And man, I don't even know what you do for a living."

"I have done a lot of things. Worked in a couple factories, tried my hand at sales—which I hated—then, when I decided to clean up my act and stop using, I worked my way through school and got a teaching degree. Now I'm teaching art at an elementary school, and I freaking love it. And I'm trying to sell some of my art, which is going pretty well, actually."

"Wow, I had no idea. You threw 'using' in there. None of my business, but did you have a problem with drugs?"

"It wasn't a problem when I was using—at least I didn't think so. But yeah. It was sort of the common story: I started using during high school. First pot, then cocaine. Also the sad and all-too-familiar story of how it was all fun and games until it wasn't. I was a mess. Fortunately, I recognized it early, got into meetings, and stopped. I was one of the lucky ones who quit pretty easily. Thank goodness."

"Wow," Michael said. "As they say at Nar-Anon meetings, thanks for sharing."

"Thank you for letting me share."

They chuckled, then Michael thought for a moment.

"You've stopped into a few lectures at BARC," he said. "But are you doing twelve-step meetings there or anything?"

"No, I was for a while, and I have absolutely nothing against that approach. I've been attending SMART Recovery meetings across town for a few years. I just found that approach resonates more for me."

"Got it. Megan covered that in one of our family meetings a few months ago, and I still have a handout about it. Heck, my folder is overflowing with all the stuff I've collected."

"I'm so glad you kept coming back to BARC," Brandon said. "We see many people come for a meeting or two and disappear. No judgment—I hope they get support someplace else. In addition to attending meetings, I've also found studying stoicism to be really helpful in my recovery and overall state of mind."

"Between you and Arnie, I keep feeling so dumb. I've never even heard of that. I know what *stoic* means, I think. Sort of like staying calm even in stressful times. And, sometimes as impassive and unfeeling. Right?"

"Yes. Good definition. No worries about not knowing about it. And you're far from dumb, pal. I'll take a shot at explaining stoicism, but my friend Sam is the one who introduced it to me, and he's an expert on it. He feels strongly that it saved him from his addictions and mental health issues. He's an open book about that, or I wouldn't have shared it. I'm sure he'll tell you all about it, if you like. I'm super proud of where he is today compared to where he was before. Just for today, though, right?"

"Sounds great. I look forward to meeting him."

"We'll be there in about half an hour. So here's my take on stoicism. It goes way back to ancient times, when it was developed by philosophers like Epictetus, Seneca, and Marcus Aurelius. It provides a way to look at life that stresses personal growth and ethical living. The word *resilience* comes up in many of the teachings. When stoics talk about resilience, they often stress the need to keep on trying, to never give up. There is a strong focus on taking action—not just sitting around talking about doing things but actually doing them."

***

Sam had obviously been watching for them, as he opened his front door and waved as soon as they pulled in the driveway. As he left, he turned back and gave a woman holding a toddler a hug, then threw them both a big kiss as well.

"Hey, Brandon, great to see you," Sam said as he jumped in the back seat. "You must be Michael. Nice to meet you."

"Likewise. Brandon told me a bit about you," Michael said. "That sure is a cute kid you said goodbye to up there."

"Thanks. That's John. He is almost two years old. He and my wife are my entire life, man! Several years ago I never thought I'd have something that meant so much to me. I'm very lucky."

"Not sure luck has much to do with it," Brandon said. "I think it's more a result of your hard work. Was it Gary Player, the golfer, who said something like that when a fan told him how lucky he was? He said, 'It's amazing—the more I practice, the luckier I get.'"

"Good point," Sam said. "I have heard that, except attributed to a baseball player, I think. But who said it isn't as important as the point. Well taken. Oh, here, before I forget. I have a 'One Show at a Time' sticker for you, Brandon. Do you want one, Michael? No pressure."

As Sam handed a sticker from the back seat to Brandon, Michael asked, "What's the sticker for?"

"They're made by a group known as the Wharf Rats," Sam said. "It's a group of people who like Grateful Dead music and who are also in recovery. I am sure you have heard people in recovery talk about 'One Day at a Time.' This sticker is a play on that saying, a way to show we can maintain our recovery one show at a time. The Wharf Rat group often has a table or a special gathering place at shows like the one we're going to tonight."

"Thanks for the explanation. I'm in recovery from my codependency tendencies, not drugs. But I'll take one if that's okay?"

"Of course," Sam said. "We're all about inclusiveness. Here you go."

"Brandon and I were talking about stoicism a bit on the way to pick you up. He said you're the expert on it."

"Hardly an expert," Sam said. "Actually, in my opinion, when we think we have something mastered, that's when we get in trouble. But, yes, I have been studying it for a while. I do think stoicism and SMART Recovery saved my life. I was addicted to heroin for way too long. I never would have had the family I have now, or a steady job for that matter, if I hadn't gotten clean."

"I often hear about someone hitting rock bottom," Michael said. "Is that what made you stop using?"

"Yes," Sam said. "But let's focus on the positive. SMART stands for Self-Management and Recovery Training. I've found strong similarities between this recovery approach and stoicism, and by combining them—well, for me at least—they seem to help me stay clean. No … not only stay clean. They help me live my best life by working on my personal growth and ethical living."

"But how is this different than the twelve-step approach?" Michael asked. "It sounds a lot like what I've learned about that."

"I agree," Sam said. "The funny thing—or sad thing, depending on how you look at it—is that there really isn't that much difference. Both focus on healthier ways of living by taking concrete action. I guess the main difference is that SMART Recovery removes the references to a higher power. But I sure wish people would focus more on the similarities than the differences—in these recovery methods and in life in general.

"SMART Recovery has a four-point program that consists of building motivation, coping with urges, problem-solving, and lifestyle balance. It also places an emphasis on something called cognitive behavioral therapy, which focuses on changing one's way of thinking and actual behaviors. Stoicism is similar, as it embraces aligning values with action and ways of living. But again, I'm all about whatever works for an individual, and I have no beef with other approaches."

"Thanks," Michael said. "I think I get it."

The three shared more about their personal lives as they got into the congested traffic approaching the outdoor stadium housing the Dead & Company concert. Brandon asked Michael if anything was new with his son or daughter. Michael said he hadn't heard from Katie for a while, which made him sad and concerned. On the other hand, he said that Billy was doing well and that they'd had a few good sessions with Billy's therapist. Billy was going to come home in a week or so, live there, and attend an intensive outpatient program during the day. Michael shared both excitement and apprehension about the upcoming change.

As they found a parking spot, which seemed more than a mile away from the venue, Michael was amazed at the number of tie-dye-clad people standing in line to get in. As they approached the screening stations, they came across a Wharf Rat banner and table. Michael was impressed that both Sam and Brandon knew several people gathered around the booth. He met a few other people and received several hugs and warm greetings. As they worked their way through the stadium, those who noticed Michael's "One Show at a Time" sticker gave him nods, smiles, high-fives, or hugs. It felt like strangers stopping strangers just to shake their hands.

***

As Brandon, Michael, and Sam made it back to their car after the show, Brandon could not resist teasing Michael a bit. "Hey, dude, I assumed you were an expert at cutting the grass in your lawn-service business, but I had no idea you were so good at cutting a rug. Those were some moves you had dancing off to the side there! Who knew?"

"I probably looked more like a dork," Michael said. "But it sure was fun.

I don't think I've danced in at least ten years!"

"You dance great," Sam said. "You know, I was a real stick in the mud about dancing up until about five years ago. I actually didn't dance at all because of what others would think. Then I read something—don't remember where right now—but I think the guy was writing about why he continued to make and promote his art. He said something about how he was going to die someday—not in a morbid sense or anything like that. It was just a statement of fact. And when he realized this, he also understood he wanted to continue to produce art. Sorry, I know that's a bit abstract, but that's when I started dancing. I just decided life was too short not to dance, and I stopped caring at all about what other people thought."

"Pretty healthy, there, Sam," Brandon said. He turned to Michael. "And hey, you seemed to dance quite a bit with that one young lady. I hope you got her phone number."

"I'll never tell," Michael said sheepishly.

Chapter 21

The dog days of August were too hot and humid for Arnie to be outside for long periods of time. QP and Merlynn were thankful for this inside time, as it resulted in many games of chess with Arnie and his family members. While appreciative of all this time out of The Cocoon, QP and Merlynn were troubled by a discussion Arnie had had with his family in his den the week before.

"Thanks for being here on such short notice," Arnie had said to his children and grandchildren, who had gathered at his request. "As a few of you know, I've been getting a bunch of medical tests done, and, unfortunately, I got some bad news yesterday. I have a pretty advanced case of lung cancer."

Arnie's daughter started to cry, then said, "You never even smoked. Are you sure? I say we should get another opinion."

"I was as surprised as you are," he said. "I learned that this disease affects nonsmokers too. It doesn't seem fair, but life often throws us curveballs, doesn't it? And I have a really good set of doctors. The tests are clear—no need to run around to a bunch of other doctors."

"When can you start treatment?" Duncan asked.

"It pains me to share this with you all, but I won't be getting any treatment. Before you object, please let me explain. My doctors and I have discussed all the options. There are a few experimental things that could be done that might extend my life by a few months, but they come with a heavy physical price, and they may not work. I have a couple months left, and I want to enjoy them with you all, not going to doctor appointments."

As they listened, Merlynn and QP were overwhelmed by the show of love and support from Arnie's family and how they came to accept his decision. However, QP was not nearly as accepting.

"I'm really sad that Arnie is so sick," QP said later. "Can't you do something about that? With one of your chants or spells or something?"

"I am sad also, but no, I cannot interfere with the circle of life. And this may sound strange, but I am thankful I cannot do so."

"Why? It seems like that would be wonderful."

"On some levels, maybe. But where would that start and stop? I mean, if I could make Arnie's cancer go away, could I then end all sickness? Would that then lead to ending suffering? To be clear, of course, I don't want any animal to suffer. But the power to stop it or change the course of events is more than I could handle. I mean, what if there were someone with an illness and I missed it? No, too much pressure for this old wizard."

"I guess I understand. You have helped me see that all things have beginnings and endings. Death is one of those endings. This reminds me of that movie we watched a while back. I think it was called *Tuck Everlasting*?"

"Ah, yes. The one where the Tuck family discovered the fountain of youth, drank from it, and stopped their aging. They could never die after drinking the water from the fountain."

"Yes. But it turned into a nightmare for them," said QP. "They couldn't have relationships, because they saw everyone around them aging and dying while they stayed unchanged."

"Good recall. What was the main lesson you took from that movie?"

"Hmm, good question. I guess it was that endings create some urgency to get things done. Sorry, that isn't very articulate. Let me try again. If everything went on forever, I think complacency could set in. Does that make sense?"

"Absolutely," Merlynn said. "Good insights. Arnie has pretty much said the same thing to his family about his pending death. Remember this afternoon when he was talking with Duncan? He said he has no regrets. He shared that he has had a very full life, surrounded by love and intrigue. It is amazing that Arnie is comforting his family through this as much as they are comforting him."

"Sorry if this sounds selfish, but what will happen to us after Arnie passes? I know you know what will happen because you are living backward and you know the future. Please tell me."

"Ah, let's just leave it at this: all will be well. Please don't worry about that, or about other things that are out of your control. And, yes, I am getting younger and younger. And, just as Arnie will miss his family, I will miss you when I transition back to the mystical wizard's womb. Let's make the best of the last few months we have together."

"I'll try," QP said. "But don't think for one minute that I like any of this! I do remember the discussions we had about the futility of worrying. I will work on putting some of those skills to use. I am curious, though, about something Arnie and Duncan were talking about the other night."

"Okay. Which discussion?"

"The one about being happy. Remember, Duncan pulled a couple of books off that shelf over there, the one with—gosh—it looks like at least twelve books on the topic of happiness."

"Yes, I see that shelf. I love looking at Arnie's full library. Notice how he has everything organized by topic. Amazing."

"I agree. So they were talking about happiness and all of those books. I wonder, what do you think about being happy? I think I'm getting better, but I still worry a lot and get upset about things. I'm not sure if I will ever be happy the way all those books talk about."

"Let's start with this," Merlynn said. "Actually, I wish the word *happiness* in all those titles were changed to *balance* or *contentment* or some similar word. Not that I have anything against being happy. I just think so much emphasis on that word creates too much pressure for people. It sets up unrealistic expectations. Striving for balance seems healthier to me."

"That makes sense. Like the yin and yang we've talked about before. I do understand that to know love and peace, one must also know pain and angst. I also remember our discussions about useless worry. I still use some of those techniques. I just feel sad at times, and I wish I knew the secret to being happy all the time."

"Ah, let me put you at ease there. There is no secret. I fear that anyone who claims to know some magic secret is misguided. There are techniques and ways to approach life that can lead to more happiness than misery. That is for sure. But there is no one answer or secret code to be unraveled."

"What are some of those steps, then?"

"I have found those who are the happiest—no, let's say the most content—are those who have purpose in life. This purpose can come from one's work, hobbies, or personal life. And having a purpose helping others is much more rewarding than having a purpose that is only self-centered. Actually, self-centered purpose usually has the opposite effect. It can lead to discontent."

"So what is my purpose, then, as a mere chess piece?" QP asked.

"First, drop the word *mere*. You are a magical chess piece destined for great things, which will become clear very soon. It is a pet peeve of mine when someone says they are 'merely' something, as if their job isn't as important as someone else's job."

"Okay. I have learned that I can, and often do, play a very important part in a game. I will try to stop putting myself down."

"Good. Also remember, even if you get captured early in a game and, God forbid, get knocked into a pool of cold coffee, you still may have played a critical part in the game. We often don't know the actual outcome of our efforts until much later. Heck, maybe even never."

QP had a puzzled look, as if she was trying to recall some previous event. "I remember reading something about that not too long ago. Oh, yeah … it was in that book *Dashboard Bagels*. It was in the chapter on the author's involvement with a group called Big Brothers Big Sisters, which connects adults with children who have no male role models in their lives. If I recall correctly, he had a match that didn't last very long, and he felt as though he had really failed that young person. Then, much to his surprise, a few years later the young man reappeared in his life to tell him how well he was doing. The moral was to not assume we have failed when we don't really know the impact we have had on others."

Now it was Merlynn's turn to get quiet with a troubled look on her face.

"You look sad, Merlynn," her apprentice said. "What's going on? Did that story upset you?"

"I am a bit troubled. Not by the story. It's a great reminder that we never know the true impact of our actions. But it made me think back to how King Arthur, in his last few years, felt as though his whole life had been a failure because he had failed in his quest to have right win out over might."

"Didn't he at least make some progress, though?"

"Yes, in the long run. Tragically, he was not around long enough to see that. I wish he and Dr. Martin Luther King Jr. had lived in the same era. Maybe then he could have benefitted from Dr. King's well-known powerful statement that 'the arc of the moral universe is long but it bends toward justice.' I think Dr. King understood that change is hard and that the pendulum often swings forward and back again."

"You were there with King Arthur. Is there anything he could have done differently to get better results in his lifetime?"

"Ah, good question. I have thought about that often over the centuries. I have no regrets, as we did our best at the time, but Arthur and I did realize something a bit late. We were trying to force people to do what we wanted. I now see the irony in that. We were trying to instill a right-over-might approach by using might."

"That I understand! We have heard stories almost every month at BARC about people trying to get someone else to do something through force, like trying to get someone to change with threats or some power move. That just doesn't work, does it?"

"No. No one will get anyone to truly change by imposing force on them. What we have seen work over and over again is that people are often influenced to change when they observe loved ones getting healthier, taking better care of themselves, and reaping the benefits of those positive actions. There's an author, Peter Block, who said this more articulately that I can in his book *The Answer to How Is Yes* when he wrote the following:

No one is going to change as a result of our desires. In fact, they will resist our efforts to change them simply due to the coercive aspect of the interactions. ... And, when we honestly ask ourselves about our role in the creation of a situation that frustrates us, and set aside asking about their role, then the world changes around us.[1]

Later in the same book, he wrote:

It is our own transformation that creates the best climate for change. ... Others ... are more likely to reflect on their own behavior as a result of our self-reflection than yield to our desire for them to be different."[2]

"That's a hard one for people to figure out, though, isn't it?" QP asked.

"Unfortunately, yes. We have heard Megan remind people of the three *C*'s of addiction many times during the monthly family support meetings. And we can add a fourth *C*, equally important. Do you remember what those are?"

"Of course! The three *C*'s of addiction for family members are 'didn't cause it, can't cure it, and can't control it.' And the fourth is that family members can 'contribute to it' if they don't work on themselves."

"A-plus, QP. Good job. I have observed that most people understand the first three *C*'s pretty quickly if they take their own recovery seriously. The fourth one—that a family member can contribute to a loved one's illness—is a bit harder. It takes a big leap of faith to trust that working on one's own recovery is one of the best hopes for their loved one to do the same."

The wizard paused for a moment. "I don't even remember what got us on this subject. Oh, yes, happiness. I think a few keys to happiness are recognizing our sphere of control, which is built into the three *C*'s, along with never losing hope and keeping a sense of humor. Hard, yes. But worth striving for, for sure."

"And we have heard Arnie say things very similar about his illness," QP said. "He understands what he has control over, and he still has a sense of humor and gratitude for his many blessings. Plus, he's actually comforting his family members as much as they are comforting him. This makes me happy and sad at the same time."

Chapter 22

Megan had a hard time calling the September family support meeting to order, as so many attendees were enjoying catching up with friends they hadn't seen for months. She eventually quieted them down enough to welcome everyone back and review the ground rules for the meeting.

Megan said the topic for the night was family structures, especially the impact of growing up as a child of an alcoholic. She listed several common impacts on a flip chart, including perfectionism, trust difficulties, rigid thinking, excessive responsibility, and anxiety.

Having had an alcoholic father, Michael was very interested in this subject. Yet he had a hard time concentrating because he was concerned Arnie wasn't at the meeting. It wasn't like him to miss a meeting, especially the first one back after a two-month hiatus. Michael had talked with Arnie a few times since the Fourth of July party but hadn't seen him since. The few times he had spoken with him on the phone, Arnie seemed tired or distracted.

Megan began by sharing her thoughts on one item on the list: that adult children of alcoholics were often rigid and inflexible. An attendee chimed in that she'd had a very hard time when plans changed at the last minute, even if the change was a good one. Megan reassured her that this was a common response and was likely due to the uncertainty of her home environment while growing up.

Michael thought about just how often things he had looked forward to as a child turned sour. Like wanting Dad to come to a school event, only to be disappointed that he didn't show up, even when he'd promised. He was coming to see that this was a reason he found it difficult to trust others.

After reviewing the other traits identified on the handout, Megan read a few sections from Janet Geringer Woititz's trailblazing book *Adult Children of*

Alcoholics. Ms. Woititz was one of the early pioneers in conducting research on adult children of alcoholics. She identified adult children of alcoholics as perfectionists and people pleasers. This really hit home for Michael.

He laughed out loud when Megan shared something Ms. Woititz had said, tongue in cheek: that it would be useful to ask applicants in job interviews whether they were adult children of alcoholics because their definition of a half day's work would be twelve hours. Though Megan stressed the facetiousness of this comment, the point was that adult children of alcoholics were often driven and dedicated to hard work. Michael was glad he'd started getting a handle on this and doing fun things for himself again.

Megan shared several other traits of adult children of alcoholics identified by Ms. Woititz, including their tendency to take responsibility for anything that didn't work out. Then, to the opposite extreme, they tended to discard anything that went well as coincidence or just plain luck.

The discussion reminded Michael of something he'd heard a friend say a while back about raising children. When Michael said to his friend that he must be very proud of his daughter's college acceptance and that it showed he must have done a good job raising her, his friend responded, "I have six children. Some are doing well, some are not. If I take credit for the ones who are doing well, then I have to take credit for the ones who are not doing as well. I choose to not do that.' While his friend had said it lightheartedly, Michael was coming to fully appreciate the wisdom in this statement as he grew healthier and more confident.

An attendee who commented said that both her parents were alcoholic and that her home growing up was so unpredictable that as an adult, she had no idea what a normal relationship looked like. Several others chimed in about having to guess at what was normal because of their childhoods. Megan noted that this was also a common trait among children of alcoholics.

Megan closed the meeting by stressing the need to avoid victim complexes as they learned more about these traits and the impacts of their upbringings. Of course children were victims in these situations, she said. But as adults, she said, the point for children of alcoholics was to learn about these impacts to inform themselves and to understand why they might act or feel in certain ways. But—and she really emphasized this—people also needed to avoid saying, "I can't change because of my childhood." That would be letting their pasts define their futures—something to avoid at all costs.

After the meeting and after he'd caught up with a few friends he hadn't seen since June, Michael approached Brandon at the reception desk.

"Hey, Artlove. Have you seen Arnie lately? I'm surprised he isn't here."

"I haven't seen him since we took our break. Actually, come to think of it, he called me last week and asked that I find someone else to lead the Nar-Anon meeting he usually leads. He sounded really tired. I hope he is all right."

"Yeah, for sure," Michael said. "Arnie is strong and stubborn, so let's hope it isn't anything serious. I talked with him last month about an issue I was dealing with, and he sounded okay." He paused. "The topic of my meeting tonight was about growing up with an alcoholic parent. It really hit home for me. I wish Arnie were here to talk about it over a game of chess."

"I don't have a chess set here, but I do have to hang at the front desk for about an hour until the AA meeting concludes. If you want to stay, I would love to talk … not that I'm as smart or insightful as that old codger, Arnie."

"I would love that." Michael sat in the extra chair behind the desk and retrieved the handout from his pocket, which was marked up with his comments as usual. Michael had circled the following traits on the handout: self-criticism, being rigid, and being overly responsible.

"Here's the handout we got tonight at our meeting," Michael said as he shared with Brandon the list of common struggles for adult children of alcoholics. "Of all these, being overly responsible hit me the hardest. I have spent so much of my life trying to figure out how I could fix everyone else. Don't get me wrong, I'm not upset about being sensitive to others' needs. That's a good thing. I just need to continually remind myself about my limited sphere of control."

"Exactly. You have made great strides in that area during the short time we've been friends. I mean, I told you when we met that we would eventually be going to a concert together. And we had a blast last month. Right?"

"For sure. That was really good for me. I am enjoying doing things for myself again."

"And those moves on the dance floor!"

"Ah, now you are making fun of me."

"No way. I mean it. I loved watching you express yourself so freely and have so much fun. As for being overly responsible, did Megan cover different roles children play within dysfunctional families? I have read much of Dr. Claudia Black's work on this. She is a noted leader in this field and often talks about four different roles children take on. I think she identifies them as the overly responsible one, the adjuster, the placater, and the one who rebels or acts out."[1]

"Yes," Michael said. "We did discuss those. As a child, I went back and forth identifying with the responsible one and the adjuster. There were times I tried so hard to fix everything. And there were times it was all too much. Times I got so tired of trying to fix everything and I just went along. I adjusted my expectations and just sort of shut down.

"Here's another thing," Michael continued. "Someone mentioned at the meeting tonight that they often felt bored or unaccomplished if they weren't dealing with some type of drama in their lives. I found this interesting because I used to feel the same way. I remember I'd come home from work and my wife would ask me how my day went. If everything went well with no emergency for me to try to solve, I often felt like the day wasn't as successful. Now, the more time I spend around BARC, and with people like you, I long for stability and the lack of drama."

"That makes sense," Brandon said. "And look at you now. You survived, and you're taking care of yourself. That is reason to celebrate. I was the kid who acted out. I did it as the family clown. I guess I kept thinking if I found reasons to make everyone laugh, they would get along better. That didn't work, for sure."

"You make me laugh all the time, so I appreciate the clown in you."

"Thanks … I guess?"

"I did mean that as a compliment. Hey, do you remember that discussion we had after the concert about my son, Billy, wanting to move back home?"

"Of course. I was going to ask what was going on with Billy and you."

"Good news," Michael said. "He came home a few weeks ago. He's attending an outpatient program during the day and seeing a therapist, and he seems to be doing very well. I love having him back home, and we're having pretty good discussions about what's going on with both of us. No drama, which is great."

"That is fantastic news. I'm happy for both of you. One day at a time."

***

They'd been chatting for about forty-five minutes when several people came by the reception desk on their way out.

"Good," Brandon said. "The AA meeting is wrapping up. I can close up soon."

Michael helped by emptying the trash cans and turning off the lights in the various rooms. As he turned the corner to leave the break room, much to his surprise, he ran right into his daughter, Katie. He was stunned to see her. He immediately fell into worst-case-scenario thinking that she'd come looking for him because of some tragedy.

Katie, knowing this look all too well, smiled, gave her dad a quick hug, and dispelled his fears by saying, "Hey. I was just leaving an AA meeting."

This brought a huge smile to Michael's face.

Before he could say anything, Katie continued speaking. "It's great seeing you, Dad. I've missed you. And I've been meaning to call, but ... well, I have a bunch of stuff to figure out. I do have some new friends waiting for me outside to go get some coffee, and ... well, I'm not really ready to talk to you yet. But I will reach out soon."

"I understand," Michael said. "I'm thrilled to see you here. For now, you do you and I will do me, and we'll look forward to better times."

"Deal."

Chapter 23

"Butt end!" Merlynn said.

"Butt end? This makes no sense," QP said. "Please don't let 'butt end' be your last words of wisdom to me. How am I supposed to make sense of that! What the heck?"

QP was understandably distraught, as she very much wanted Merlynn to help her process the fact that Arnie was dying. She had not dealt with death before. Unfortunately, Merlynn's metamorphosis back to infancy had come much faster than QP had expected.

Just in the past two weeks, Merlynn had lost most of her ability to put sentences together. While she had difficulty using language, she still had all of her senses, so she found it very funny when QP mistakenly thought she had said "butt end." Though enjoying this joke immensely and slightly tempted to let QP go through the next several centuries carrying "butt end" as her last piece of guidance, Merlynn's better nature won over, and she found the strength to clarify.

"No, not 'butt end.' Both/and!"

"Ah, 'both/and.' That makes much more sense. We have talked about 'both/and thinking' several times. Isn't that right? Merlynn? Come on, Merlynn, I was hoping for more from you while you are still able to communicate with me. I have learned a great deal in the year since you brought me into awareness, but I am not ready yet for you to leave me."

Alas, Merlynn did not respond. She just looked off in a different direction and giggled.

As Merlynn sat silently fiddling with her pacifier, QP reflected on a memory from a few months before, when she had doubted Merlynn's magical nature.

***

QP had asked the wizard, "You were just talking about a time you changed Arthur into a fish as part of his studies. You also said you have been a queen in this chess set for as long as you can remember. How can that be? While I confess to being confused, I think you are even more confused."

"Yes, it is very possible that I am confused," Merlynn had said. "I am not troubled or disturbed at all if I am. Humans are so uncomfortable with the thought that they could be confused. They want to seem so certain of everything. I think this is a dangerous habit. I think it much healthier to admit we may not know everything. Unfortunately, throughout history, people are seldom rewarded for admitting that they don't know something. I wish this were different.

"It makes me very sad that people dismiss those with different ideas or beliefs so quickly without even considering they might have something of value to add to each other's lives. I have seen so many humans, fish, birds—just about any creature you can think of and even those beyond your wildest imagination—miss great learning opportunities because they refuse to be confused. They are not willing to truly consider a new opinion or idea, as they are so convinced they are right."

"You haven't answered my question," QP protested. "How could you be with King Arthur in medieval times and also elsewhere at the same time? That seems impossible."

"I have been in several different forms at the same time. Our understanding of time is so very limiting," Merlynn said. "I don't mean this to be critical. It is just where many of us are on our evolutionary cycle. Fortunately, this silly idea that time is fixed and only moves in one direction is expanding as we gain a better understanding of complex topics like quantum physics. While I find that a fascinating field of study, it would be too much to delve into in the limited time we have left together.

"All I ask for now, QP, is that you suspend your thinking that something cannot exist in many different forms at the same time. Please trust me. I am living proof. I am here with you now and I am also many other places as we speak."

***

Both/and thinking was a tough idea for QP to wrap her bulb around. At times she thought it was just made-up talk. She still felt things should be one way or the other. Black and white. Not all this paradoxical stuff.

As QP struggled with the concept of both/and thinking, she recalled another discussion she'd once had with Merlynn about it. Merlynn had told the pawn about a thought experiment conducted with several human audiences that always had similar results.

***

The experiment went like this. The moderator asked the group if they considered themselves to be law-abiding citizens. The answer was pretty much universal: "of course." The moderator followed up by asking where the participants set their cruise controls while driving in zones with sixty-five-mile-per-hour speed limits. As expected, hardly anyone set their speed at or below sixty-five miles an hour. Even though the people considered themselves to be law abiding, in fact, they broke the law almost every time they drove on highways.

"This thought experiment often hit a nerve with audiences," Merlynn had said. "Some participants said things like, 'Oh, bull, everyone speeds. No way does that make me a criminal. This is a dumb example.' But I like a thought experiment that hits nerves because that is when some of the best learning takes place.

"I like this example, as it shows we all engage in some hypocritical thinking. Or maybe *hypocritical* is too strong a word. How about *paradoxical*? Yes, I like that term better. The point is that if we can let down our defenses long enough to take an objective look at our own conflicting beliefs, we might be less critical of others. And while we are doing this, we can also remember to work on being less hard on ourselves. Try to grant ourselves grace.

"I like this Buddhist saying I heard over a century ago: 'Act always as if the future of the universe depended on what you did, while laughing at yourself for thinking that whatever you do makes any difference.' This is a good example of both/and thinking. It feels paradoxical, but life is full of paradoxes. We do great harm to ourselves when we fight against paradoxes rather than accept them."

***

QP drifted back from reminiscing and tried to get Merlynn to say something, but the wizard remained unresponsive. To escape this new reality, QP returned to recalling memories from a few months ago when they had been on the chess board with Michael and Arnie. Arnie had been talking about the importance of metaphors in life.

"Michael, as you know well by now," he'd said, "many of the stories I share with you contain metaphors. For example, Jonathan Rowson—you know, the guy who gave me this chess set—often spoke about chess as a metaphor. He talked about metaphors being a very important part of our intelligence and stressed that the lessons of chess were important ones.[1] By working on ourselves, by accepting our paradoxical nature, by embracing metaphors as great tools of learning, that is how we can keep being creative, how we stay lifelong learners."

On another occasion not too long ago, Merlynn had said to QP, "As my ability to communicate with you is waning, please remember this of all the things we have discussed since you became aware: the work ahead of you can be very serious at times. Equally if not more important, you do not always have to be so serious. Make your moves wisely and with care, for yourself and for all of mystery's creations, as you have fun playing the game. You are ready for greater things, and you are well prepared. You have been an able student to a fare-thee-well."

Even now, QP still wasn't sure what work Merlynn had been referring to that could be so important. Unbeknownst to her, she would understand soon enough.

She'd been feeling more confident after spending several months with Merlynn, but insecure thoughts occasionally came back to haunt her. Fortunately, these thoughts were more fleeting than they'd been before.

She thought back on a discussion Merlynn had shared with her that she had overheard between Mr. Rowson and Garry Kasparov, arguably one of the best chess players ever. This discussion happened as they were putting the pieces away after a game of chess. They were discussing stereotypes, and Mr. Kasparov said something like it being important to not listen to the stereotypes we have of ourselves. He stressed that our own opinions of ourselves were often wrong, and often we didn't give ourselves enough credit. He further stated that if we listened to these negative thoughts, they could become self-fulfilling.[2]

QP was thankful for these reminders about learning to value her own abilities and self-worth. She found she needed to continually draw on them to avoid slipping back into destructive negative self-talk. While she felt a bit more confident, she still longed for more from her mentor.

"Hey, Merlynn? How can I best put both/and thinking into action? What should I do next? Can you help me with that?" Unfortunately for QP's rising desperation, the now very young queen merely grabbed for her pacifier.

QP cradled Merlynn in her arms. (Well, she would have ... if pawns had arms.) She gazed into Merlynn's face, hoping to draw out any last words of wisdom from her sage.

As she sat on the chess board in the book-lined den, distraught over Merlynn's condition, Arnie and Duncan entered. She noticed Arnie was moving much more slowly and was having difficulty garnering enough energy to speak.

***

As they sat down on opposite sides of the chess board, Arnie said, "Duncan, see all my chess books on the third shelf down over there?"

"Yes."

"Please go and grab the one ... I think it's the fourth one in. The one titled *All the Wrong Moves*, by Sasha Chapin."

"Got it. Here you go, Gramps."

"Thanks, ah, here it is," Arnie said as he flipped through the many dog-eared pages. "I wanted to share this exchange between the author and Ben Finegold, a chess grandmaster. Finegold told Chapin, 'You have to play like you never want the game to end.' In turn, Chapin wrote, 'And he was right. I didn't believe him. But I asked him to tell me more.' So Finegold explained:

"In life, and in chess, people make terrible decisions just because they're impatient. They want things to end, right now, on their terms. They just want a reckoning, whether or not it's actually good. ... But you don't have to play that way. You can play for hundreds of moves, if you want to. You could play for a thousand. And if you're happy with that, your opponent will be like, I want a sandwich, I want a beer, I want to get out of here. But meanwhile, you're content. You don't have to go anywhere. You just like moving the pieces around. You just like playing chess."[3]

Arnie continued. "I read this many years ago and am glad I did. I have loved every minute of this life, every minute with you and other family members, and every minute of moving these pieces around. I don't think I have this spelled out in my will, Duncan, but I want you to have any books in my library that you would like to keep."

"Wow. You know how much I love books. I got that from you, even though I still cringe when you dog-ear a page! As long as you are sure, I will gladly take all of them. They will always be my most cherished possessions."

"Thank you for that. But don't hang on to them too tightly. I have probably given away as many books as are in this room. Sharing with others brings untold rewards. Now, let's play. Let's see you put that math knowledge to work."

Duncan sensed, though he did not know for sure, that this would be his last game of chess with his beloved grandfather.

Chapter 24

Michael had learned of Arnie's illness a few weeks earlier and was devastated at the thought of losing his friend. He could not bring himself to attend the October meeting at BARC knowing Arnie's parking space would be vacant. Rather than attend the meeting, he called Arnie to see if he was up for a visit at home. Although Arnie sounded weak, he said he'd love a visit, especially since there was someone there he really wanted Michael to meet. After confirming he wouldn't be interfering with the other visitor, Michael headed across town to Arnie's home.

"Hey, Grandpa told me you were coming," Duncan said as he opened the front door. "He's looking forward to seeing you."

"Good to see you," Michael said. "I loved our discussion about game theory a few months ago, although my head is still spinning from it. Maybe we can chat about it again sometime. How's your grandfather doing?"

"Not good, really. He's tough, as you know, but not well."

They embraced, holding back the tears, as Duncan led Michael to the den. Michael was both surprised and pleased to see Arnie engaged in a game of chess with his visitor.

"Michael, I'm so glad you came over. This is Father Rohr … Richard Rohr. He's a good friend and has been my spiritual advisor for many years now. I'm sure I've mentioned him to you before. He came all the way from New Mexico to visit."

Arnie turned and grabbed a sealed envelope and handed it to Duncan. "Here, take this. This is what I want on my headstone. Don't you let those fuddy-duddy kids of mine stop you. Got it?"

"I promise, Grandpa," Duncan said. He took the envelope and left the study.

Father Rohr rose and gave Michael a warm handshake and a hug. "It is nice to meet you. Arnie has told me about you. He thinks very highly of you. While he didn't get specific, he shared how much you have grown and embraced your own recovery the past year or so. Congratulations on that."

"Thank you, Richard ... I mean, Father." Michael said. "Sorry, I'm not good at religious stuff. I'm not very spiritual. I hope Arnie didn't tell you that. Maybe I should start over."

Father Rohr chuckled. "No worries. You are among friends here, and there are many forms of spirituality and worship. You are here visiting an ailing friend. That is a wonderful way of celebrating the human spirit. And you have been working on your growth, which is another form of spirituality whether you call it that or not. You have been transforming your pain into action, and there is nothing more spiritual than that."

"Please sit, Michael," Arnie said. "We are just wrapping up our game. Let me finish off the good Father here as we chat."

"We will see about that," said Father Rohr as he moved QP into a position where Arnie couldn't stop him from anointing her a queen on the next move.

Meanwhile, Goofus, having never been around a man of the cloth, was so intimidated that he crawled under Michael's collar and hid.

Realizing he was about to lose the game, Arnie looked the Father in the eyes. "So, do you feel good about beating a dying man?"

Seeing how uncomfortable Michael looked at this statement, Arnie said, "Michael, please don't worry. Yes, I don't have much time left. And I'm truly okay with that. Of course, I will miss you, my family, being around BARC ... but I have had a good long life. No one gets out alive. That's part of the deal.

"And you know me well enough to know"—he winked—"that I won't let tonight pass without laying more of my favorite quotes on you." He paused. "I love what Mark Twain said about death: 'I do not fear death. I had been dead for billions and billions of years before I was born, and had not suffered the slightest inconvenience from it.' While I'm not sure what lies ahead, I do have faith it will be something good."

Father Rohr interjected, "the human ego prefers anything, just about anything, to falling, or changing, or dying. The ego is that part of you that loves the status quo—even when it's not working. It attaches to past and present and fears the future."[1]

"I have learned a lot about change and acceptance from you, Father," Arnie said. "I think you once shared with me that everyone loves change, as long as it is their idea. I love your sense of humor, especially about challenging topics."

Arnie turned to Michael and handed him a book. "Michael, before I forget, I asked Father Rohr to bring you a signed copy of his book, *Falling Upward: A Spirituality for the Two Halves of Life*. It has meant a great deal to me the past few years. I hope you like it."

"Wow," Michael said. "Thank you! I'm sure I'll love it."

"Actually, before you came over today," Arnie said, "we were sharing some of our favorite ideas from his book." He grabbed his copy from the side table and flipped through the pages. "Right here in the introduction, the good Father uses this quote from The Odyssey: 'Death is largely a threat to those who have not yet lived their life.'[2] I couldn't agree more."

"I am so glad my book has meant so much to you," Father Rohr said as he grabbed his own copy and looked for a passage. "That reminds me of something else on point for this discussion. Where is it? Okay, here on page seventy-eight. 'Only that which is limited and even dies grows in value and appreciation; it is the spiritual version of supply and demand.' I have sat by many as they took their last breaths. Those who are most at peace with this unavoidable change are those who have lived full lives."[3]

"I love how you put thing, Father." Michael said. "Arnie, one of the many things I've learned from you this past year is the importance of living a full life. Of taking risks and appreciating even the hard times, as they often result in the greatest growth."

"Thank you for sharing that, Michael," Arnie said. "And you're still a young man—well, compared to me, at least. This stuff does take time."

"Before you arrived, Michael," Father Rohr said, "we were also sharing ideas from this book"—he tapped on a book on the side table—"by Richard Leider and David Shapiro, *Claiming Your Place at the Fire*. It's about becoming 'new elders,' as they call it, about sharing wisdom we've gained over lives well lived, about giving back. They talk about their belief that new elders know that death is a profound teacher and that death is actually what gives life meaning.[4] Now, to be clear, that doesn't mean we don't yearn for more time, especially with our loved ones, with friends. Of course we do. But we also learn to accept things as they are."

"Good point," Arnie said. "The authors also talk about keeping a sense of humor. If I recall correctly, they talk about the need to embrace the absurdity of life, to not take ourselves and everything so seriously all the time."

"We sure have had several good laughs together, Arnie," Michael said. "But I still find all of this overwhelming. I'm not sure I'll ever get to a place of peace with you leaving. Or that I will know as much as you two do."

"Well," Father Rohr said, "I hear you and understand your doubt, but please remember this isn't a competition. Don't compare yourself to others. I sense deep insights from you in the short time we have been together. A solid spirituality, even if you don't claim that word. And feeling overwhelmed and confused is part of the process. Part of being human. We are often not in total control of what happens around us."

"I get the 'not being in charge' part," Michael said. "I don't claim to know much, but I think I've gained a good understanding of the Serenity Prayer, of knowing what I have control over and what I do not. I credit this guy right here with helping me with that." He gestured toward his friend and chess partner.

"Thank you," Arnie said. "Speaking of not being in control, I would love to continue our visit, but I'm really tired, and I need some sleep. Before you go, Michael, here ... let's put these chess pieces back in their bag. I want you to take this chess set we have used so often as a gift from me."

When Michael objected, Arnie said, "I insist. This is part of my getting closure. I can think of no one I'd rather give this to. When Grandmaster Rowson gave it to me, he encouraged me to pass it along to someone who would make good use of it. Please accept this."

It so happened that when Arnie picked up Merlynn and QP, he said, "I don't know what it is, but I think there is something magical about this chess set. Sorry, Father, I don't mean in some secret spiritual way, or anything like that. At times, it just seems as though I feel a power or presence of something greater than myself from this set."

While Merlynn could no longer respond verbally, QP clearly saw her wink as Arnie said this. Suddenly, QP's angst about what would happen to them after Arnie passed away vanished, as she knew they would be in good hands with Michael.

"No need to apologize to me," Father Rohr said. "I firmly believe there is much in life that we don't understand. My friend James Hollis said this better than I can in his book *Finding Meaning in the Second Half of Life*. He wrote, 'The world is more magical, less predictable, more autonomous, less controllable, more varied, less simple, more infinite, less knowable, more wonderfully troubling than we could have imagined being able to tolerate when we were young.'"[5]

Arnie looked over at Michael. "Here's one final thought about aging I recall from *Claiming Your Place at the Fire*, Michael. The authors quote the wonderful Danish philosopher Søren Kierkegaard, who said something like, 'Life can be only understood backwards, but it must be lived forwards.'[6] Go live your life forward, with gusto, with passion, recognizing that some of it may not make sense until much later when you look back on it from a distance."

At hearing about understanding life backward, not only did Merlynn wink at QP, but she also conjured up a smile.

Chapter 25

Arnie's memorial service was a beautiful celebration of a life well lived. While Michael felt worn out emotionally, the mid-November snowstorm was not about to keep him away from BARC after attending the memorial service earlier that afternoon. Tears ran down his face as he slid into a parking spot. His stomach churned as he looked at Arnie's now-vacant handicap parking place. He still couldn't believe his friend was gone.

As he worked on stopping the tears, Michael reflected on the wonderful eulogy given by Duncan and the other heartfelt tributes to Arnie. Duncan had made several references to his grandfather's passion for life, love of people, and positive attitude.

Duncan also talked about Arnie's love for chess. He asked those who had met Arnie through the game of chess to stand. Michael couldn't even count the number of people who stood, but it must have been well over forty. Then— though surely it was just his imagination— Michael could've sworn he felt a special vibration of energy coming from the chess bag on his lap, which he'd brought to the funeral. Though he didn't know it, Merlynn and QP appreciated Michael's thoughtfulness in taking them into his care.

His sadness turned to laughter as he thought about the graveside service after they'd left the church. Just as Arnie would have wanted, the afternoon ended on a light note, with Duncan reading Arnie's last words and unveiling the headstone.

"Last month, Grandpa gave me a sealed envelope with instructions for what he wanted on his headstone," Duncan said. "He also asked me to read this. So here goes. 'Hi. Arnie here. Thanks for coming to my service. Yes, my children, as expected, I am going to get in the last words today. So, let's close by paraphrasing these words from one of the greatest philosophers ever, Doctor Seuss: 'Don't cry because it's over. Smile because it happened.' Please keep this thought with you as you think back on my life and our interactions. I love you all."

Duncan stepped up to the headstone and removed the covering. Chiseled into the granite was a quote by Will Rogers: *Lead your life so you wouldn't be ashamed to sell the family parrot to the town gossip.* As they left, the attendees walked through the graveyard with smiles, just as Arnie had planned.

Some days, the eleven months since he'd read the flyer in the grocery store about BARC's family support meetings felt like eleven years to Michael. Other days it felt like eleven minutes. He'd learned so much in that short amount of time.

As he sat in his truck composing himself, he noticed a gentleman he didn't think he'd seen before standing outside the front door of BARC. He appeared to be hesitating. Michael recalled his own reluctance to attend his first meeting.

As Michael exited his truck, he reached across his front seat and grabbed Arnie's chess set. Technically, it was his chess set now, but he would always think of it as Arnie's chess set. He doubted there would be anyone to play with, but he knew he wanted to have the set with him to give him the emotional support to get through the meeting.

As he approached the door, the person who had been lingering outside started to head back to the parking lot. With his attention focused on this unfamiliar person, he didn't see the patch of ice and wound up flat on his back. As he hit the pavement, the chess pieces scattered all over the parking lot, sliding on the ice.

Michael thought Arnie had come back from the grave when he heard the echo of Arnie's first words to him: "Hey, you okay? That was quite a swan dive you just took. Can I help you up?"

Michael looked up and realized it wasn't Arnie speaking but the stranger he'd seen walking away from BARC. "I think I'm okay. This is just a habit I seem to have when this parking lot is icy. Let me gather myself a bit."

Brandon pulled into the parking lot alarmed at the sight; he was pretty sure his friend Michael lay flat on his back while another man stood over him. As he eased into a parking space, he thought he felt a small bump, as though he'd run over something. Something very small. Little did he know Goofus had flown off Michael's shoulder and bounced into the space he'd just pulled into.

Seeing the headlights approaching and the tire a few inches away from him, Goofus' last words were, "Ah, shit, I hope there is no karma." Gallant saw his counterpart get squished and felt bad for him—for a fleeting second before the sense of relief took hold. While not knowing why, Michael also felt a welcome lightness of being shoot through his entire body as Goofus became a mere spot on the pavement, a spot only Michael could see.

Gallant thought about Arnie's graveside service and mused about things he could have etched on Goofus' headstone. Then he recalled a piece of guidance he tried to follow: "If you can't say something nice about someone, don't say anything at all."

Brandon hurried over and confirmed his suspicion that it was Michael, still on his back. "Are you all right?"

"Yes, I just slipped. I think I hit my head. Let me rest just a bit longer."

As Michael composed himself, Brandon and the stranger picked up a few of the scattered chess pieces. At they reached down to help Michael up, it so happened that Brandon held Merlynn and the stranger held QP. When they joined hands with Michael, something magical happened. The energy of the connectivity between them surged through Merlynn, reviving her ability to communicate with QP one last time.

Merlynn made time stand still as she asked, "QP, can you hear me through the vibrations in Brandon's hand?"

"Yes!" QP said. "Wow, what's going on? I love hearing your voice again. I have missed it. But I'm confused."

"Understandably," Merlynn said. "The synergy of the three humans holding hands—two people helping another—revitalized me. Listen closely, as I don't want to keep them frozen too long in this weather. After this, I will be making my final transition, but I think I can conjure up a few last spells. I have an idea of what to do, but I don't want to proceed without your consensus. I have too much respect for you to do that. What would you like as my last act?"

"How about for you to not leave?"

"We talked about that before. Sorry, but that is still out of my control."

"Okay, how about to make me like you, then? To give me your skills, power, and sense of security?"

"I am honored," Merlynn said. "That is something I can do. Let's start with the sense of security part. I have wanted to make up for screwing up my original chant when I brought you into awareness and making you so codependent. I mean, clearly you have mostly overcome that, but I think I know how to build on what you have already accomplished.

"Several years ago, I read a wonderful book by Melody Beattie, *Codependent No More*. I know we have talked about that book at times. Let me pull that from my memory bank. Okay, here it is. I am going to transfer all the knowledge and wisdom from this book into you. While I'm at it, I am going to implant it in our friend Michael as well.

"Here we go. I sure hope this works. TOIL, TOIL, FOG AND BUBBLE, HELP QP AND MICHAEL SEE THAT WHEN WE TRY TO CONTROL OTHERS, WE ARE ONLY ASKING FOR TROUBLE." Merlynn got it right, and QP felt a sense of confidence and peace of mind she had never felt before.

"Wow," QP said. "I am still tingling all over. Thank you."

"You are welcome. We are not done yet. You have become a queen several times in games. Would you like to make that change permanently, recognizing that we always leave something behind when we make significant strides? You will no longer be a pawn and will take my current form."

"I can think of nothing I would like more. I am ready."

"Good. Nothing would make me feel better than transferring all my knowledge and magical abilities to you. I won't be able to use them in the womb anyway. Would you like that as well?"

"My goodness, yes. It is a bit scary, though."

"As it should be. With power comes a great deal of responsibility. But I know you will use it wisely. Please remember to take care of yourself as you help others. You will be no good to anyone if you get burned out. And your mission is not to save people. Your task is to open their thinking to new ideas."

"Thanks. I have learned that from you, from Arnie, and from Michael. I will remember that well."

"Okay. I will miss you, but it is time for me to go. Oh, sorry, one more thing. I think you need a new name. You can hardly be Queen's Pawn as a queen yourself. Any ideas?"

Yes! I want to be Queen CoNoMo!"

Seeing Merlynn's puzzled look, QP explained, "I am feeling the surge of confidence from absorbing the 250 pages of *Codependent No More*. My new name, Queen CoNoMo, uses the first two letters of each of the three words in the title."

"I love it! Farewell, Queen CoNoMo!" With that, Merlynn cast her last spell, unfroze the three humans, and vanished into the void of the wizard womb.

Michael, Brandon, and the newcomer found themselves holding hands in the cold. They had no idea they'd been frozen still, but they did have a sense that something special had just happened. Especially Michael, who felt more confident and assured than he ever had.

"Are you sure you're okay?" Brandon asked.

"Yes. Strangely, I feel fantastic. More confident. How strange is that? I hope it's not just a concussion." He turned to the stranger. "Hey, thanks. What's your name?"

"John. No problem. Here's the chess pieces I picked up. I'm glad you're okay. I need to get going now."

"Hold on there, John," Michael said. "Sorry if this is too direct, but I noticed you standing outside when I was sitting in my truck. Were you just leaving another meeting?"

"Oh, no. I was thinking about going in for the family support meeting. But I'm not sure this place is for me."

Michael chuckled. "This feels like a flashback," he said. "Almost a year ago, I was right where you were. I was going to leave, but someone convinced me to give this place a try. Someone who changed me for the better in ways I can't even begin to explain. Can I talk you into coming in?"

"Well, you are pretty convincing. I guess I have nothing to lose. I really don't like being at home anyway, these days."

"Trust me. I know the feeling. I used to feel the exact same way. Not anymore, though, thankfully. Come on, let's get out of this cold snow and rain."

As they walked toward the front door, Michael's cell phone rang. "Oh, hi. Great to hear from you, Sarah. Yes, I am well. Listen, can I call you back a bit later? I'm just headed into my meeting. Cool. Talk later."

Brandon couldn't help but tease his friend. "Sarah?"

"Yes. The woman I danced with at the Dead & Company concert."

Brandon smiled widely as he held the door open for Michael and John.

As they passed through the front entrance of BARC, John said to Michael, "I love playing chess. Is there any chance you'd have time for a game after the meeting?"

From within The Cocoon, Queen CoNoMo smiled.

141

Acknowledgements

This book would not have been possible without the unwavering support and encouragement of my spouse and best friend, Joy Wilson. Her valuable insights and honest critique greatly improved this book. Thanks also to our son, Duncan Wilson, for his assistance.

I also owe a deep debt of gratitude to my development editor, Julie Miller, with The Editorial Department. She corrected my tendency to over-write with grace and patience. She also questioned my logic in a number of areas and did a masterful job of making the story flow more smoothly.

Editing assistance was also provided by Dan Mager, author of two books: *Some Assembly Required: A Balanced Approach to Recovery from Addiction and Chronic Pain* and *Roots and Wings: A Guide to Mindful Parenting in Recovery.* Dan read my entire manuscript and offered valuable input.

Thanks also goes out to friends Jim McCormack and Robin Tabora who read various drafts and provided their thoughts and inspirations. And to friends, Brandon Athey and Michael Chamblee, for permission to use their first names and certain aspects of their lives and of our friendship in my book.

Finally, but no less important, a thank you to everyone who played a role in my life – my many mentors, teachers, counselors, and those who believed in me when I did not believe in myself.

Amor Fati!

Notes

Chapter 2
    1. Beatty, *Codependent No More*, 36

Chapter 3
    1. White, *Once and Future King*, 46.

Chapter 5
    1. Franklin, "The Morals of Chess,." 1.
    2. Rowson, *Seven Deadly Sins*, 106.
    3. Rowson, 112.
    4. Rowson, 112.
    5. Rowson, 110.

Chapter 6
    1. Rowson, *The Moves That Matter*, 16.

Chapter 7
    1. Block, *Answer to How*, 78.
    2. Franklin, "The Morals of Chess." 2

Chapter 8
    1. Soltis, *Wisest Things*, 58.

Chapter 9
    1. "Lincoln as a Chess Player," *The American Chess Magazine*, 1897, excerpt from "Honest Abe – Chess Player," https://www.chess.com/article/view/honest-abe, May 24, 2015.
    2. Soltis, *Wisest Things*, 18
    3. Eugene Brown's ABC interview, date unknown, permission granted by Mr. Brown
    4. Big Chair Chess Club (website), accessed April 5, 2024, https://bigchairchessclub.org/.

Chapter 10
    1. Soltis, *Wisest Things*, 132.

2. Soltis, 132.

Chapter 11

1. Lessing, *Marriages Between Zones*, 156.
2. Kasparov, *How Life Imitates Chess*, 181.
3. White, *Once and Future King*, 129.

Chapter 12

1. Mel Pohl, "The Brain Disease of Addiction," *Nevada Lawyer*, November 2020, 24.
2. Northern Nevada Business Weekly, May 23, 2012 – "Doctor explains to attorneys the 'rat brain' urges behind addiction."
3. ibid.
4. Pohl, 24.
5. ibid.

Chapter 13

1. Zander and Zander, *The Art of Possibility*, 78.
2. Eauchice, "Funny 12 Steps," Sober Recovery forums, June 10, 2015, https://www.soberrecovery.com/forums/friends-family-alcoholics/369330-funny-12-steps.html.
3. Rowson, *Seven Deadly Sins*, 50.

Chapter 14

1. Boss, *Ambiguous Loss*, 61.
2. Boss, 134.

Chapter 15

1. Black, *Undaunted Hope*, 58.
2. Black, 9–10.

Chapter 16

1. Rohr, *Falling Upward*, 114.

Chapter 17

1. "The Inauguration of Franklin D. Roosevelt," National Park Service,

updated January 16, 2021, https://www.nps.gov/articles/000/franklin-roosevelt-inauguration.htm.

2. Peter Doggers, "Nelson Mandela - The (Small) Chess Connection," Chess.com, updated December 9, 2013, https://www.chess.com/news/view/nelson-mandela---the-small-chess-connection-4257.

3. Soltis, *Wisest Things*, 230.

Chapter 21

1. Block, *Answer to How*, 21.
2. Block, 115.

Chapter 22

1. Black, *It Will Never Happen*.15

Chapter 23

1. Rowson, *The Moves That Matter*, 12.
2. Kasparov, *How Life Imitates Chess*, 73.
3. Chapin, *All the Wrong Moves*, 211.

Chapter 24

1. "Top 400 Richard Rohr Quotes (2025 Update)," QuoteFancy, https://quotefancy.com/richard-rohr-quotes.
2. Rohr, *Falling Upward*, xxxvi.
3. Rohr, 78.
4. Leider and Shapiro, *Claiming Your Place*, 131.
5. Rohr, 25
6. Leider and Shapiro, 17.

Bibliography

Beattie, Melody. *Codependent No More: How to Stop Controlling Others and Start Caring for Yourself.* 1st ed. Hazelden, 1987.

Black, Claudia. *It Will Never Happen to Me.* 1st ed. Hazelden, 1981.

Black, Claudia. *Undaunted Hope: Stories of Healing from Trauma, Depression, and Addictions.* Central Recovery Press, 2024.

Brown, Brene. *The Gifts of Imperfection: Let Go of Who You Think You're Suppoed to Be and Embrace Who You Are.* Hazelden, 2010.

Brown, Eugene, and Marco Price-Bey. *From Pawns to Kings!.* Eugene Brown, 2016.

Block, Peter. *The Answer to How Is Yes: Acting on What Matters.* Berrett-Koehler Publishers, 2003.

Boss, Pauline. *Ambiguous Loss: Learning to Live with Unresolved Grief.* 1st ed. Harvard University Press, 2000.

Boss, Pauline. *The Myth of Closure: Ambiguous Loss in a Time of Pandemic and Change.* W.W. Norton & Company, 2021.

Chapin, Sasha. *All the Wrong Moves.* Anchor Books, 2020.

Chodron, Pema. *Comfortable with Uncertainty: 108 Teachings on Cultivating Fearlessness and Compassion.* Shambhala Publications, 2002.

Franklin, Benjamin. "The Morals of Chess." *The Columbian Magazine*, December 1786.

Hanson, Rick, and Richard Mendius. *Buddha's Brain: The Practical Neuroscience of Happiness, Love, and Wisdom.* New Harbinger Publications, 2009.

Heath, Chip, and Dan Heath. *The Power of Moments: Why Certain Experiences Have Extraordinary Impact.* Bantam Press, 2017.

Horowitz, Israel A. *Chess Openings: Theory and Practice.* Simon and Schuster, 1964.

Horowitz, Israel A., and Fred Reinfeld. *Chess Traps, Pitfalls, and Swindles: How to Set Them and How to Avoid Them.* Simon and Schuster, 1954.

Kahneman, Daniel. *Thinking, Fast and Slow.* Farrar, Straus and Giroux, 2011.

Kasparov, Garry. *How Life Imitates Chess: Making the Right Moves, From the Board to the Boardroom*. Bloomsbury USA, 2007.

Leider, Richard and David Shapiro. *Claiming Your Place at the Fire: Living the Second Half of Your Life on Purpose*. Berrett-Koehler. 2004.

Lessing, Doris. *The Marriages Between Zones Three, Four, and Five*. Flamingo, 1994.

Neff, Elliott. *A Pawn's Journey: Transforming Lives One Move at a Time*. Made for Success Publishing, 2018.

Rohr, Richard. *Falling Upward: A Spirituality for the Two Halves of Life*. Jossey-Bass, 2011.

Rowson, Jonathan. *The Moves That Matter: A Chess Grandmaster on the Game of Life*. Bloomsbury Publishing, 2019.

Rowson, Jonathan. *The Seven Deadly Chess Sins*. Gambit Publications, 2001.

Senge, Peter M. *The Fifth Discipline: The Art and Practice of the Learning Organization*. 1st ed. New York Doubleday/Currency, Chicago, 1990.

Shenk, David. *The Immortal Game: A History of Chess*. Doubleday, 2006.

Soltis, Andrew. *The Wisest Things Ever Said About Chess*. B.T. Batsford, 2008.

Ruiz, Don Miguel. *The Four Agreements: A Practical Guide to Personal Freedom*. Amber-Allen Publishing, 1997.

Russell, Bertrand. *The Conquest of Happiness*. Liveright Publishing, 1930.

White, Terence H. *The Book of Merlyn*. Shaftesbury Publishing Co., 1977.

White, Terence H. *The Once and Future King*. Ace Books, 1987.

Zander, Benjamin and Rosamund Stone Zander. *The Art of Possibility: Transforming Professional and Personal Life*. Harvard Business School Press, 2000.

Made in the USA
Las Vegas, NV
09 May 2025